EVERYONE DIES FAMOUS
IN A
SMALL TOWN

**BONNIE-SUE
HITCHCOCK**

faber

Content Note: One of the many story strands in this novel is connected to sexual abuse (not graphic), which may be a sensitive issue for some readers.

First published by Wendy Lamb Books, an imprint of Random House US, in 2021
First published in the UK in 2021
by Faber & Faber Limited
Bloomsbury House, 74–77 Great Russell Street
London, WC1B 3DA
faberchildrens.co.uk

Typeset by M Rules
Printed and bound by CPI Group (UK) Ltd, Croydon, CR0 4YY

A CIP record for this book
is available from the British Library

ISBN 978-0-571-35042-1

6 8 10 9 7 5

To those who do not know that the world is on fire,
I have nothing to say.

BERTOLT BRECHT

ALASKA

• Gina and Poppy

• Camp Wildwood
Amy, Fiona and Lillian

BRITISH
COLUMBIA

MONTANA

• Lared
Kelsey

~~California~~
Sea Shaken

• Martha and Jane

• Delia GUM

WASHINGTON

WYOMING

• Jenny

• Granville
Conrad † and Ben

COLORADO

• Pigeon Creek
Ruby and Jake

Louise

Nate and Finn

Angry Starfish

Gina pushed the metal snow shovel across the ice, carving a path that she and Poppy could then skate on. Well, if Poppy would quit whining and get her skates laced. Somehow Gina had gotten roped into taking her dad's girlfriend's kid to the pond. She'd only relented because it was minus twenty outside and Poppy had looked horrified at the idea. Her dad's getting a new girlfriend had given Gina's anger a whole new lease on life.

Until recently, she'd thought it had been waning, but mostly it just smouldered inside her rib cage. It was exhausting, being herself, fighting so hard all the time. She had been almost ready to just give up and let it all go. 'Moving on' was what her counsellor called it, and Gina wondered if she meant they should pack up and leave town, start over somewhere that did not remind Gina so much of her mother.

Instead, the girlfriend, Libby, had arrived with her cute little daughter, and *poof!* It was as if someone had thrown kerosene on Gina's smouldering briquettes of anger. She could feel the flames leaping, the heat licking her sternum. On really cold days, it was almost nice.

'Sure, I'll take Poppy over to the pond to skate,' she heard herself say. 'We could even hitch Alpaca up to the sled and have him pull us over.'

Alpaca was their oldest husky – her mother's favourite – and the trip would take twice as long with him. Gina smiled smugly to herself, thinking of her otter-fur mittens that never let the cold get anywhere near her fingers. Poppy's, she'd noticed, were down and Gore-Tex, no comparison to animal skins.

Her dad, though, had smiled at Poppy and said, 'You know, I think we have some of Gina's mittens from when she was little that you should wear. And I'll put the caribou hide in the sled so you stay toasty warm.' Then, to make matters worse, he'd even given her the fur hat Gina's mother had sewed while her hands were still able to pull the needle through the stiff leather on the inside.

That was a long time ago, before the disease had attacked her mother's joints. By the end it had kept her from even writing her name. Gina wished she could forget the image of her mom's bent fingers gripping a stubby pencil as if her life depended on signing her name one last time. That image was all Gina had left, unless you counted a father who would move on with another woman and smile sweetly at that woman's daughter. Maybe he thought Gina was a lost cause because she had read a book through the funeral, refusing to look at anyone or anything, especially the casket. She hadn't known what else to do.

All she had really wanted was for someone to tell her it was okay to fall apart, but nobody did.

The disease was the reason her mom had stopped harnessing up the dogs to go to the corner store, the same one that Gina pulled in to on the way to the pond while Poppy sat in the sled, talking to herself.

'What did you say?' Gina asked, stepping off the runners to tie Alpaca to the post.

'I was talking to Elizabeth.'

'Who's Elizabeth?'

'She's my best friend. She's right here.' Poppy patted the empty seat beside her.

Gina blinked at Poppy and felt her lashes sticking together, moisture freezing them in tight crystals. She put her fur gloves over her eyes for a couple of seconds until the crystals melted and she could prise her lashes apart. But Poppy was still all alone, sitting in the sled.

She had overheard Libby telling her father about Poppy's invisible friend. 'We think it's her way of coping...'

But then they'd noticed Gina standing in the hallway. Libby put on a fake smile and changed the subject.

Gina refused to ask her father anything, preferring instead to ignore Libby's appearance in her life because ignoring things was Gina's superpower.

She really didn't care if Poppy had invented a friend to fix whatever she needed to 'cope' with. Gina had her own things to deal with and didn't appreciate having someone else's kid dumped in her lap. Or her dogsled.

'Whatever,' she said. 'Stay here. I'm going to get a treat for Alpaca.'

Inside she walked toward the wooden wine barrel full of dog biscuits that sat in the middle of the room. Honestly, the place was nothing more than a log cabin pop-up store that catered to locals, so dog treats were the best-stocked item, followed by Twinkies, motor oil, herring bait in the summer, and assorted whiskeys all year round. The prices were ridiculous, though. Who needed a toothbrush bad enough to pay ten bucks for it? Her dad had carved her one out of a carrot once, telling her to make do until they could go to the bigger store in town, where things were much cheaper.

Just pushing open the door and walking inside had made Gina miss her mother so much she thought she might have to sit down. Would she ever not be overwhelmed by this place? It was one of her oldest memories, them coming here together on the sled. But it was such a long time ago she felt silly that her legs still reacted this way, going all wobbly beneath her.

Before Gina had been even Poppy's age, her mom had stopped putting her on the caribou skin in the bed of the sled and stopped laughing at the way Gina hid her face when the poop came flying out of the dogs' butts as they ran, her little head just at the right height for the smell to come wafting back into her nose.

Gina had loved it when the sled had swung up onto the snowbank, and she'd leaned side to side, afraid to fall out but also not, because she could hear her mom's crisp, high laugh saying it was okay; nothing bad could happen to her while they were together.

And when they got to the store, Oliver, the owner, who had the spikiest whiskers anybody had ever seen, would give Gina a hot chocolate and she'd melt her eyelashes over the steam. Then she'd ask for an ice cream, and everyone thought that was hilarious, which made Gina feel like she'd said something clever, but she didn't know what.

'Why, hello there,' a voice said somewhere behind her shoulder blades, knocking her back to the present and making her turn around, hoping to see Oliver smiling at her like the Ghost of Christmas Past.

But Oliver had died years ago, and this new version of him was thinner, way more clean-shaven. And he was smiling at someone else.

Poppy had followed her inside, even though Gina had told her to wait in the sled.

'Elizabeth was cold,' Poppy said to both the man, who was already handing her hot chocolate in a Styrofoam cup, and to Gina, who looked like she wanted to throttle her.

'We aren't staying long enough for hot drinks,' Gina said, aware that nobody was pouring cocoa for her. 'And there is no Elizabeth.'

'She didn't mean that,' said Poppy to the empty air beside her. The man smiled at the space just beyond Poppy's right ear and genially played along. 'Hello, Elizabeth. Would you like some cocoa too?'

Poppy giggled. 'She's a mermaid,' she told the man, blowing on her drink. 'Her tail was starting to freeze outside, so I brought her in. When she warms up, she can grow legs, and then she can ice-skate with me and Gina.'

She smiled at Gina as if they were best friends. The man seemed to find all this incredibly charming. Gina wanted to barf.

'My niece runs a summer camp down on the Peninsula,' he said. 'Maybe come summer, you and Elizabeth would like to go for a week or two?'

Why would anyone pay money to be in the outdoors? Gina wondered. Then she worried that maybe she'd said it out loud.

'You could make some friends. Maybe Elizabeth would meet some other mermaids too,' he added.

Oh, for God's sake.

'We should get going,' said Gina. 'What do we owe you for the cocoa?'

He waved his hand in the air, batting her question away.

'Mermaids and lovely young ladies always drink on the house.'

Gina grabbed Poppy roughly by the shoulder and dragged her out the door. She noticed that Poppy's right hand was determinedly clutching the air, as if Elizabeth would be left behind if she let go.

'I would appreciate it if you listened when I told you to stay put,' she hissed.

'But Elizabeth needed to thaw out her tail.'

Gina untied Alpaca as he nuzzled her hand for the treat. She turned back to see Poppy climbing into the sled and then lifting the air with both hands and setting nothing into the seat next to her. She gently wrapped the caribou hide around the empty space, whispering into the cold air so her breath looked like cartoon bubbles hovering over her head. 'It's okay. If your legs don't grow back in time, you can keep your tail tucked under this hide and sit in the sled while we skate.'

Alpaca started to pull them forward and then loped into a run, making Gina squint into the cold, gratefully feeling her eyes begin to tear as they picked up speed.

The only thing she could appreciate about Elizabeth just then was that Alpaca was unfazed by the extra passenger.

At the pond Gina threw on her skates, grabbed the shovel, and set off to clear the ice. For all she cared, Poppy could catch up or she could just sit there and keep talking to Elizabeth about rainbow houses and cotton-candy pillows and whatever the hell else nonsense the girl was on about.

Gina glided out onto the ice and felt the connection of the frozen water beneath her metal blades. She'd been skating all her life, and the movement itself was a welcome escape from her overworked brain. She leaned into it with everything she had, floating across the pond's surface as she cleared herself a path.

She didn't know how long she effortlessly skated and shovelled, skated and shovelled, skated and shovelled, like a meditation – until Poppy's voice slowly reached her out on the middle of the pond.

'Gina, my hands are frozen. I can't get my skates on. *Help!*'

Goddammit. Poppy was still sitting in the sled, her stocking feet wrapped in the caribou hide.

What the hell do you know about frozen fingers? Gina thought, pushing away the image of the pencil, the mangled claw like a chicken's foot clutched around it.

She skated backward over the path she'd just

created, dragging the shovel behind her. Gina was an expert at skating backward, almost as if her feet had known that life was going to look better in reverse and somehow she could manage it more smoothly in retrospect. Her knees slightly bent, she flowed across the ice like butter melting in a hot skillet, her blades etching curvy lines into the crust of the pond – the sound, calming her down, helping her forget. Until she got back to where Poppy sat.

'Why did you take your damn mittens off?'

'They're too big,' Poppy whined, her eyes wide on Gina's face, as if she thought Gina might explode. Well, it was certainly possible.

Gina threw off her own mittens and threaded Poppy's laces through the holes with lightning speed. It would take only seconds for her hands to freeze, too, so she had to be fast.

'Okay, quick. Get your feet in there.'

Poppy's feet looked round, like an elephant's, in four pairs of woollen socks, one of which Gina's mom had knitted her years and years ago. She closed her mind to keep out any image resembling knitting needles and long, slender, healthy fingers.

'Greta says you remind her of a starfish,' Poppy was saying.

'A what?'

'A starfish.'

Gina had forgotten that Greta and Poppy were cousins. Greta was a few years older than Gina, but they often tried out for the same dance parts, and the competition between them was historic. In truth, since Greta was older and the better dancer, it hadn't made sense for Gina to get the better parts, but Greta missed a lot of rehearsals fishing with her granddad every summer.

If Gina worked hard, she often landed roles that should have gone to Greta. Gina had been so competitive and maybe more than a little smug about it. But that was before.

After her mom died, Gina had simply been cast in the lead roles and nobody said anything anymore about tryouts. It bothered her, but if she complained, then what? Would someone ask her to talk about how she felt? She hated that they gave her the cherished leads – pity roles? – and then stared sympathetically at her while she danced.

In a small town, you are forever defined by the worst thing that ever happened to you.

And just like her mother dying, she didn't know how to stop it.

'How am I like a starfish? That's ridiculous.' She thought it might have something to do with the word 'star' being misapplied, but Gina was surprised as Poppy ploughed on, unaware that she might be treading dangerously close to the thin ice that was Gina's temper.

'Greta says starfish are actually bad.'

'Well, isn't Greta just an expert on everything.'

'No, I mean bad for the fishermen. Starfish eat the bait off their hooks.'

'How is it that I'm eating anyone's bait?'

Gina had no idea where this was going. And it was getting cold sitting in one spot.

'Poppy, we have to skate. We're going to freeze.'

'Okay.'

Poppy wanted to hold her hand and Gina knew it, but she skated off before that could happen. Backward. She watched the younger girl struggle to get her stride in Gina's old skates, which were too big despite all those socks. The beaver-skin hat kept slipping over Poppy's eyes, so every two seconds she had to push it up again. The girl was drowning in animal fur. What would Libby say if Gina brought Poppy back as a wriggling beaver and said she didn't know how it had happened? Maybe Libby would be furious and never come back to their house. Gina wouldn't mind if Libby stayed away, especially at night.

She hated thinking of Libby in her mother's bed, changing the smell of the sheets and pillows. She didn't care what her father did with Libby; she just wanted him to do it somewhere else, because she was starting to forget her mother.

The sheets had always smelled like lavender and mint and wet dogs. Bits of dog hair clung to everything because the washing machine was full of dog hair, so even clean, all their laundry was furry. But once Libby had started staying over, the sheets smelled more like coffee and chocolate and some flower Gina couldn't identify.

Sometimes Gina sat in her mother's closet and breathed in her clothes, which was like sitting in a bog near ripe, low bush cranberries, because her mom had spent so many hours picking that smashed berry juice permanently saturated her sweaters and the knees of her jeans. But that too was slowly fading; it had already been over a year. As long as there was a hint of mouldy cranberry emanating from that closet, maybe her mom would never really be gone.

'Wait up, Gina!'

Poppy skated clumsily, chopping at the ice as if her skates were axes. Gina slowed and made lazy figure eights, waiting for her. When Poppy caught up, Gina relented and grabbed the girl's hands, hoping to pick up the pace. 'How am I like a starfish?' she asked, wishing she didn't care.

Poppy was panting and holding hard to Gina's wrists. 'Well, if you chop a leg off a starfish, it just grows back. And if you chop it in half, it will grow two bodies.'

Gina stared at her. 'So?'

'Well, Greta said the fishermen who are green – you know, the new ones? They don't know this. When they pull the gear up on their lines, if the hooks are full of starfish that ate all the bait, the fishermen get so mad they chop up the starfish and throw them back overboard. But instead of solving the problem, they've just doubled it.'

'I still don't follow.'

'She just said that you're so angry, you're like a starfish. You chop off one bit of your anger and then it grows back, twice as big.'

Gina was livid that Greta was talking about her as if she could possibly know what Gina felt. She dropped Poppy's hands so hard her mittens fell to the ice, leaving the little girl's fingers exposed and throwing her so off balance that she toppled onto her butt, her bare hands flat against the frozen pond. Poppy started to cry, but Gina skated off toward Alpaca and the sled, leaving Poppy to crawl around on her own to find her mittens.

It was the winter solstice, the shortest day of the year, and Gina realised it was already getting dark. Off in the distance, a flash of colour glistened across the snow. Alpaca had suddenly pricked up his ears and taken notice. Perhaps it was some kind of hare or ptarmigan; if so, he'd be after it like a shot.

Gina had unhitched him from the sled, which he seemed to have only just realised as he started to run, untethered, toward the shadow that every once in a while glinted against the white backdrop. She tried to untie her skates but her hands were too stiff, giving Alpaca a good head start, and he would not listen when she called. She shoved her feet into her snow boots and chased him, still clutching the snow shovel.

The snow got deeper in a hurry, making her plunge through the top crust, slowing her down, and still all she could hear was Poppy's ridiculous little voice telling her that she was a starfish. Her anger exploded. It grew a leg, and then another leg, and then a body.

She could feel her angry starfish body growing bigger and bigger, and suddenly she was swinging all her starfish arms and legs, now numbering in the twenties, the thirties, the forties. She was a starfish monster swinging at everything in her path. The whole world seemed to be screaming, egging her on, louder and louder as she swung her pointy arms again and again and again.

And then she was lying on her back – the screaming had morphed into deathly silence – while all around her the snow glistened with colour. Shards of red and purple and glassy green were everywhere, as if a rainbow trout had flopped around, scattering its lovely scales. As her eyes adjusted, she realised it was just the aurora reflecting off the white, white snow. She had been the one doing all the screaming.

Gina was so tired. Her shovel lay next to her, still gripped tightly in her otter-skin mitten. She saw it as if from a distance and tried to let go, but her hand had become a claw; she couldn't flex her fingers. For the first time she thought about how much pain her mother had been in. What a relief it must have been to be free from an earthly body that would not do what it was intended to do.

I'm so sorry, I'm so sorry, I'm so sorry, Gina said to no one and everyone, but mostly to her mother, who was maybe one of those stars blinking overhead, and then finally to Poppy, who had made her way over all on her own, miraculously dragging the sled by Alpaca's empty tug line.

Frozen snot covered Poppy's face, and her eyelashes were caked with ice from tears that had frozen before they could fall.

Finally Alpaca came back and curled up on one side of Gina as Poppy curled up on the other, and they huddled there, slowly warming themselves against each other's frozen bodies.

'Poppy, are your hands okay?'

Above them, the lights changed from the green of a mallard's head to the soggy grey-green of pea soup.

'They're cold,' said Poppy.

'Put them under my coat,' said Gina. 'I can thaw them out.'

'It's okay. Elizabeth is holding them.'

Gina rolled over and looked at Poppy's hands lying at her sides. They were two balled-up fists clenching the empty air.

'Well, Elizabeth can still hold them if you warm them on my belly. She doesn't have to let go.'

'Okay.' Poppy sniffed. 'She'd like that.'

Gina helped Poppy get her frozen hands out of her mittens again. The little girl's fingers were turning white, and Gina braced herself for the icy touch against her stomach. She carefully covered them with her shirt and then her coat, trying not to press on them too hard with her own mittened hands. *Please be okay, please be okay.*

'I should have never left you on the ice like that,' Gina whispered. 'I'm sorry, Poppy.'

'It's okay,' said Poppy. 'Elizabeth was there.'

Pigeon Creek

Ruby was no shrinking violet. She knew Jake was sneaking off in the night, but she didn't know what she could do about it. She knew it, not because he would have otherwise been sneaking into her house – God, her father owned hunting rifles! – but because he was suddenly perpetually yawning. His eyelids were constantly drooping over his sea-foam-green eyes, like two sagging window shades blocking a view of the beach.

She would have been hard pressed to miss something like that, even from landlocked Colorado.

Ruby loved Jake's eyes more than anything else about him because they were uncomplicated. Even when she'd been very young, before she'd understood what a crush was, Jake's eyes had made her giddy, as if she could swan-dive into them.

But they also always gave him away.

'You look beat,' she said, tossing her homemade felted backpack into the backseat of his white VW Bug.

Every other teenage boy in Pigeon Creek owned a pickup truck and used words like 'gas guzzler', 'big bed', 'bucket of bolts', and other manly terms to describe their alter egos. Jake was not like the other boys in Pigeon Creek. He was confident enough to drive around in a car called a Beetle, for starters.

Her father watched from the kitchen window. Ruby said nothing to Jake about the fight they'd just had, how her father had said that her music was awful and to turn it down.

'What are you trying to do, dance with the devil?' he'd asked tersely.

He could have been talking about her music or her boyfriend, actually.

She didn't tell Jake that she'd slammed the door in her father's face. She didn't need to widen the chasm between Jake and her father. Truthfully, she would have liked it if they got along. She loved her dad. Usually, their relationship was not a door-slamming kind. But it seemed they were both feeling edgy these days.

Jake yawned and didn't respond to her comment about how he looked. Lately, much of what Ruby said barely registered with him, as if he was always somewhere else, even when he was sitting right next to her.

'Dad says you should get the muffler fixed,' she said as he turned the key in the ignition.

Right on cue, at the sound of the muffler,

Priscilla – or was that Ophelia? – lifted her head from the blackberry brambles that clung to the wooden fence. Ruby's father's goats were the only things that could tame the ornery plant.

Ruby marvelled at the idea of a mouth that could chomp blackberry thorns like a Weedwacker.

And then for no reason other than she was suspicious, Ruby thought about Martha Hollister. Martha had a mouth like a Weedwacker, *and a body like a hooker*, said a little voice in the back of her head.

Martha also swore like a sailor, laughed with teachers like they were her peers, and ignored the boys in her class at Pigeon Creek as if they were grapes withering on the vine. Probably because she had thickets of ripe, juicy, thorny boys somewhere else to snack on. Martha was only a sophomore, and yet Ruby knew that sophomore Martha Hollister had already made her way through the entire class of eligible senior boys at Pigeon Creek High School. Everyone knew.

Jake was not eligible, but what happens when you've finished with all the blackberry bushes, the ones you were *allowed* to have? Well, if her father's goats were any example, you moved on to the perennial patch or even the clothesline. Nothing was off limits. Ophelia had once gorged herself on Ruby's father's long red woollen underwear and hadn't even choked on the buttons.

God, Martha Hollister, you indiscriminate little goat.

Ruby glanced over at Jake, but he was concentrating on driving through half-open eyelids. She had an urge to grab the roll of duct tape from his glove box and use it to tape his eyelids to his forehead. He'd had a whole extra hour of sleep yesterday because they'd turned the clocks back for daylight savings time. What the hell?

He'd also forgotten to kiss her good morning.

Jake could see Ruby squirming in the seat next to him, even though he could barely keep his eyes open. He liked to joke about how he could drive around Pigeon Creek blindfolded, but the truth was, even old people who'd spent their whole lives in this town couldn't do that. The town was an obstacle course of right angles, and the only thing that saved people from dying on blind corners was the fact that the speed limit was something like negative ten. People here didn't drive: they crawled.

He wanted to tell Ruby, but every time he thought he was really going to do it, she'd do something so sweet and familiar he couldn't bring himself to lower the hammer. That was exactly how he thought of it: as lowering the hammer and shattering everything they'd shared over the past four years. And all the years before that, if anyone was counting. He'd known Ruby all his life.

His best friend was sitting next to him, bouncing

around like she had to go to the bathroom, and he knew exactly what she was thinking. She always wriggled when she was mad and didn't know how to tell him. That was love, wasn't it? All of it: the knowing, the not talking, the weird moving around in her seat . . . How do you just walk away from that?

But then, how do you not sneak out and tap on the window of a beautiful girl who's willing to do anything – *anything* – when you're a teenage boy who can't see straight because you're bored out of your mind living in a town the size of a peanut, driving like a senior citizen? It was 1995, but Pigeon Creek was stuck in a time warp. Of course you're going to go off the rails sooner or later.

Martha Hollister was the fast-moving train that had come to town so the boys of Pigeon Creek could realise that speed limits are simply *suggestions*.

But the thing he really wanted to tell Ruby about was the moose.

Until last night, Jake had only ever seen moose in the national park. But at 2 a.m., lying naked next to Martha in that strange bottle gazebo her mother had grouted together in their backyard (who *were* these people?), he had heard the sound of alders being pulled from the ground and the chomp, chomp, chomping of a moose having a midnight snack.

Jake had wondered briefly if glass bottles were

enough of a barrier between them and an angry mama moose – he did not want to die naked – when he'd jumped up to see just how close they were and peered out through a square Bombay Sapphire gin bottle that was just at his eye level. The brown eye staring back at him from the other side looked like a cold, wet marble. It blinked, and then from somewhere deeper came a low, rumbling cacophony of regurgitated alders. The moose had actually *burped*. Then it turned unceremoniously and went back to chomping branches.

Martha, lying naked on the grey woollen blanket spread out across the dirt floor, had laughed like a hyena.

Ruby wouldn't have laughed like that. But Ruby wouldn't have been naked on the cold ground either.

By the time he pulled into the school parking lot, he knew he would ditch his first-period class to go sleep and he would not tell Ruby that he was ditching class, or that he'd snuck out to visit Martha Hollister. Or, worst of all, that a burping moose had made him remember his girlfriend while he was messing around with someone else.

Ruby was normally the only person he could talk to, but certainly not about this and definitely not now.

Because as Ruby got out of the car and swung her bag (why did she have to felt everything?) over her shoulder, he saw her staring at Martha Hollister, who had just walked up to the kerb with boots that were too high, a skirt that was too short, a laugh that was too loud.

Martha glanced over at Jake and then coolly ran her eyes over him as if she owned him. She might as well have shouted through a megaphone. Ruby saw it and instantly she knew. And Jake knew she knew. Why were girls so goddamn telepathic?

Martha tried to rearrange her face, but it was too late. She hadn't meant to do it, honestly she hadn't. Especially since the last thing she saw when she turned to walk nonchalantly past the flagstone with the words 'Pigeon Creek High School' etched on it (Lord, why was every sign in this town etched in flagstone?) was Ruby throwing her felted bag back inside the car. Had she actually hit Jake in the side of the head with it before getting in herself? He did not look at Ruby, nor did he look at Martha. He stared straight ahead, like a man going to his own funeral.

Martha heard the door slam and then she heard the muffler, the same muffler she strained to hear late at night. Even though Jake parked a block away, that rattly sound like fate laughing at its own joke was her cue to dab a tiny bit of gardenia perfume on both her wrists and behind her ears, the very middle of her neck. In the time it took to do this, two quick taps would sound on her window. It had become practically

27

routine; why shouldn't she glance at Jake at school as if she could eat him for breakfast? They'd been doing this all summer, and he said he was going to tell Ruby anyway. The clock was ticking.

The perfume had been a going-away gift from her friend Jane when she left California. Nobody here had it. The girls here wouldn't have known what to do with gardenia perfume, if Martha was being honest.

That's right, *honest*, not mean.

Martha wrote Jane letters about Pigeon Creek and Jane wrote back, 'Oh my God, you poor thing, you have stepped back into the 1940s.'

But Martha didn't feel sorry for herself. She was the most thrilling thing to happen to Pigeon Creek in years, and that was not lost on her. She floated down the hallways of her new school like a fairy from a foreign land as the denim sea parted to let her through (cowboy boots and cowboy hats, denim jeans and jackets – she'd never seen so much denim in her life), knowing she was turning heads with her knee-high leather boots and her shimmery short skirts.

Martha had told Jane when she left that she was going to take this place by storm. And by God, she had.

The only problem was Ruby. If Martha had been more charitable, she would have felt sorry for the token hippie of Pigeon Creek, but she could only shake her head and laugh at the idea that felting everything wool a person owned and wearing clothes like billowing circus tents made you a hippie. And then there was the fringe. God, So. Much. Fringe. But worse, Ruby wore her hair in two long braids. How old was she, five?

It didn't help that Jake had been dating Ruby, the hippie wannabe, for years before Martha had arrived in Pigeon Creek.

History is a difficult thing to dismantle, unless you're a dictator.

Glancing at them in Jake's VW Bug – a car she had never ridden in herself, now that she thought about it – Martha thought she might actually love Jake. He wasn't like any of those other boys, and there was something both thrilling and terrifying in that realisation. If she loved him, then she had something to lose, and that scared her more than anything.

Okay, maybe she shouldn't have given him 'the look'. She would apologise tonight when he came by. Maybe he was cutting it off with Ruby right now. Because Jake loved Martha back, didn't he? Well, she would apologise anyway. She slid into her desk and pulled out her Webster's dictionary, also a gift from Jane.

Apology: a written or spoken expression of remorse, sorrow or regret for having wronged, insulted, failed or injured another.

Hmmm, that didn't sound right.

Next definition: *Apology: An inferior specimen or substitute; makeshift.*

Yes, that was it. Ruby was a sad apology for a girlfriend. Jake was going to dump her any minute.

Martha told herself again she was just being honest, not mean. She closed the dictionary and flipped her hair forward, adjusting her headband, aware that all her classmates' eyes were on her as they filed into the room.

She would have felt guilty if she had anything to feel guilty about.

Jake drove Ruby in silence, unsure where they were heading. There weren't a lot of options – this was Pigeon Creek, after all. And since Jake was having the worst day of his life, of course Ruby's father just happened to be walking down the sidewalk toward them. Oh God, it was like a slow-motion train wreck.

The closer they got, the deeper the frown line in her father's forehead grew. Ruby gave him the tiniest nod to say she was all right but not great. Her father's radar for her was so finely tuned, he'd pull Jake out of the moving car and beat the shit out of him if she gave even the smallest indication that it was warranted.

Jake certainly deserved it. But no, she'd deal with him herself.

'Keep driving,' she said. 'Whatever you have to say, it would be best to say it far from my father.'

Even if she was heading away from school, her dad

trusted her. He'd know she had a good reason. She'd explain later.

Jake had hoped Ruby would ask him to just take her home. Since she already knew what he was going to say, why make a big dramatic play of it? She could have told her father she didn't feel well and Jake had helpfully given her a ride home, although even he was aware that of all the things Ruby was now thinking about him in the passenger seat, the word 'helpful' was not one of them.

He drove the speed limit, so slowly his eyes were locked the whole time with her father's until he finally slid past and it was safe to blink again. There was something a little incongruous and downright creepy about staring into your girlfriend's eyes and seeing her father, but it was even creepier the other way around.

Especially if you'd done something wrong.

Ruby was such a daddy's girl. That was another thing he appreciated about Martha Hollister: no looming father figure to make his life difficult.

For the second time that morning, Jake felt like he was heading to his own funeral.

And then he did the worst thing he could possibly do under the circumstances: he *laughed*.

Ruby stared at Jake, confused by the sound coming out of him. She had nothing in her vast arsenal of emotions to turn to, so she just stared at him like she'd never met him before.

31

Should she yell? Punch him? Grab the wheel and kill them both?

Her gaze was blistering.

He could feel the heat coming off her.

He coughed and cleared his throat.

'I'm sorry,' he said unconvincingly. 'Sorry I laughed.'

'You're sorry you laughed?'

'And I'm sorry I hurt you.'

'But you aren't sorry for what you did, are you?'

He said nothing.

'What exactly did you do, Jake? And how often?'

'Oh, Ruby, come on . . .'

She wanted him to say it. She wanted him to describe in sickening detail every single transgression.

He wasn't even decent enough to do that.

They were near the quarry now. The trees lining the narrow road were laden with fruit. It was that time of year when all the over-ripe apples and plums falling from the branches would pile up in the ditch – a fruit salad for wasps. They drove past a dead raccoon in the middle of the road, still cradling a smashed crabapple in its equally smashed paws, flat against the pavement.

The quarry trucks caused so much roadkill.

There's a metaphor, thought Ruby as Jake's tyres spun over the bodies of hundreds of flattened green toads.

She glanced in the rearview mirror. Shadows danced across the backseat.

'What are you looking at?' Jake asked, relieved to reduce everything to this moment. To ask a seemingly simple question.

'The light is playing tricks,' said Ruby, who was also happy that there were still simple questions with simple answers, in spite of everything.

Except it wasn't simple. The shadows made her imagine Martha Hollister lying across the backseat, her short skirt hitched up to her waist. Ruby thought her brain might explode. How long had Jake been playing her for a fool?

She stared again at the side of his face as he drove, marvelling at how it was possible to know a person so well and not at all, in the very same breath.

Somehow he had slipped away, this boy she'd known forever.

She missed who they had been at the ages of ten, twelve, and especially fourteen, when all the possibilities were suddenly split wide open like a piñata that had been smacked repeatedly in the hallways of Pigeon Creek Middle School by a bazillion hormones whacking away at it on their way to class.

Back then, the hair on her arms bristled just from being close to Jake, from the electric shock of all the possibilities, especially the ones they hadn't even known existed.

In health class, the jaded, middle-aged Mr

Spatchcock (really, that was his name), his round rutabaga face tinged pink, went on and on about their changing hormones, how it happened to everybody, how normal it was – 'Nothing to get all worked up about!' he had practically shouted above the din of thirty students whose blood was all rushing loudly in their ears, drowning him out.

But it had been special to Ruby.

Those *changing hormones* were obviously going to mean more for the kids of Pigeon Creek, because nothing much ever happened here.

They *needed* it to be special.

Even the camp songs they'd known their whole lives and sang at the top of their lungs, even these had become flirtatious and loaded with innuendo once they'd hit puberty.

Don't throw your trash in my backyard, my backyard, my backyard. Don't throw your trash in my backyard, my backyard's full.

Ruby remembered how Jake would croon her favourite round in a falsetto, as if his underwear were two sizes too small. And then one day in the lunch line, completely out of the blue, it had sounded totally different.

Fish and chips and vinegar, vinegar, vinegaaaaaaaaar ...
Fish and chips and vinegar,
Pepper, pepper, pepper, salt.

That day, with pointy elbows jostling her in the ribs and the smell of the bleach solution the lunch ladies sprayed on the tables surrounding her, his voice had resonated, deep and manly, and those last four words had taken Ruby's heart with them.

The warmth that spread all the way into her toes was so unexpected, she thought everyone must be able to see it. Like when she'd peed her pants in preschool (but hopefully not exactly like that).

The plastic utensils wrapped in a scratchy brown napkin; the meat, rice and gravy blending into the soggy green beans; the carton of chocolate milk: it had all suddenly smelled stronger and felt heavier in her hands.

She'd barely been able to walk to her seat without tripping.

It had seemed so easy when she was fourteen and had handed Jake her heart right there next to the chicken fried steak on her blue plastic lunch tray, no questions asked.

In four years she hadn't thought twice about it, until now.

Now she wondered why singing about condiments had made such an impression on her anyway.

Pepper, pepper, pepper, salt. Really?

Sitting next to Jake now in his stupid little car, tiny dead animals making a thump-thump-thumping sound under the tyres, Ruby realised that the only thing that stood out about that day now was her blue lunch tray and the way the gravy had jiggled when she walked, like greasy grey Jell-O congealing on her plate.

Maybe Mr Spatchcock had been right: it was nothing special. She had just wanted it so badly.

Recently, every once in a while, Ruby had gotten a whiff of something foreign coming from Jake when he was close to her. Something like oiled leather, something sweet and flowery, the tiniest hint of a smell that she'd actually *liked*. She had thought he was using some new soap; she had thought he was making some kind of effort; she had thought he loved her. God, she was a first-class idiot.

She hadn't been able to place that flowery scent. And even though she still had no idea what it was called, she was certain where it had come from.

He had been telling her they were over, but never with words. Instead, he'd used a shrug, or a look, or that mysterious smell, and she had ignored all of it. He had been lying to her for months, and now all he could do was laugh.

She switched on the radio in time to hear the latest update from Coyote Jones, the local weather guy.

'Fire danger is at its peak, folks. No campfires. No burn barrels. I wouldn't even venture to barbecue a steak in this weather. And if you're feeling particularly in love, take a nice long skinny dip in the river. Do not even think about rolling in the hay.'

Normally, Ruby thought Coyote Jones was hilarious, but not today.

'You bastard,' she said, slapping Jake so hard across the side of his face that he swerved into the opposite lane.

'Holy shit, Ruby, what the hell?'

'I will never forgive you.'

The VW careened around the corner, flew onto its side, went over the bank and rolled a few times. It was like she was watching a movie of her life in slow motion. What had she just done? The world was spinning, and she heard herself screaming for her mom, who she hadn't seen in months. She'd told herself she didn't miss her mom and her sister, but that was a lie too. Maybe the truth was that Jake didn't feel like being the only solid thing in her life, as Ruby's family fell apart around her.

FLIP: she saw her sister Poppy's wide terrified eyes. FLIP: she heard her mother yelling at her father. FLIP: Poppy's best friend went missing. FLIP: her parents split up. FLIP: her mother moved to Alaska with her little sister. Every rotation of the car conjured another terrible thing that had happened.

Her head banged against the dashboard; stars swirled in her brain. The car landed on the creek bank, rocking like a turtle flailing around on its back.

Ruby had said she was staying with her father so he wouldn't be alone. Hadn't she really chosen staying with Jake – the lying son of a bitch – over leaving with her mom and sister? The last thing she saw before the car finally stopped spinning and the world went deathly silent was Martha Hollister's knee-high leather boots as she walked into Pigeon Creek High School like she owned it.

Then the faces of the people Ruby loved hovered around her like ghosts, mixed with the smell of diesel and burnt rubber. She must be dead. What a relief, dying before anyone could find out what had happened.

She and Jake would be the famous high school sweethearts memorialised forever in a deadly car crash. Because everyone dies famous in a small town, don't they?

From the window she saw fuel leaking out of the VW, dark and oily and flowing down to the riverbank. Ruby wiggled her fingers and toes. She didn't feel dead.

Jake was hanging upside down next to her, both of them secured just by their seat belts. She reached over and touched his arm, surprised at how calm she was. He opened his eyes. She let out her breath.

The blood in her ears had nothing to do with love this time, just gravity. She thought of her mom and Poppy and how much she missed them. Her mother had wanted to start over somewhere else, and for the first time Ruby understood how that felt. Her father wouldn't mind letting her go, especially if it meant getting away from Jake. She had heard that Alaska had more coastline than any other state. She would finally see a real live crashing ocean.

Martha Hollister could have Jake's eyes; she could drown in them, for all Ruby cared.

They helped each other out slowly, silently, checking for broken bones. She had a lump on her forehead; he had a cut on his cheek.

Jake sat down next to her on a rock and they stared at the overturned car. He wasn't laughing now.

'You could have killed us,' he said.

'How, Jake? You already did.'

Sea-Shaken Houses

Martha Hollister wasn't really from California at all.

But saying so wasn't a total lie, because the place where she grew up sat on the edge of the Pacific Ocean – just like California – and Martha's brain was bendy enough to make that work.

When she was younger, Martha and her best friend, Jane, had loved growing up in this place they called Sea Shaken. It was a spot on the stretch of beach along the coast of Washington and British Columbia that was too beautiful to even be named on a map, so they had named it themselves. Everything there was sea shaken: the houses, their badass mothers, and especially the smell of the salty air.

For Jane and Martha, it was all they had ever known, mingled with a mystery that kept them busy exchanging clues from things their mothers said about a man neither of the girls had ever met.

Did they possibly have the same father?

'He wore a dirty white hat,' Jane reported, after her mama had let that slip one night while she stirred the cheese packet into the macaroni. Martha's mother used real, grated cheddar when she made macaroni and cheese, and she let the girls call her by her first name, Zoe.

They both called Jane's mom Mama.

It was a rare slip, this bit of info, and Jane had immediately run to Martha's to tell her.

'Got it,' Martha had said. 'I'll check Zoe's diaries for anything about a white hat.'

'Dirty white hat,' Jane corrected her. Details were important.

Martha had been reading Zoe's diaries for years and reporting back to Jane, not once thinking that this might be considered snooping.

They had tried asking direct questions, but neither Mama nor Zoe was forthcoming. The dirty white hat was like a golden ticket in a chocolate bar.

'He wasn't from here, Jane,' was all Mama would ever say, as if that were a real answer.

Not from here? thought Jane. *Nobody is from here.*

The fact that their mothers were both tight-lipped only reinforced what the girls wanted to believe. And it helped that their imaginations had been sharpened to fine points in an isolated place with very few other people and hours and hours to kill.

They were both homeschooled (if you asked Jane's mama) or unschooled (if you asked Zoe), meaning they were free to roam the ocean's edge, be curious, study whatever they fancied. For Jane, it was bivalve molluscs, clams, mussels, anything with a shell that spit and squirted. She spent hours digging them up, cutting them open, dissecting their kidneys and hearts, fascinated by their siphons and eager to know how they functioned. By the time she was twelve, she knew almost everything there was to know about them. So did Martha, but that was only because Jane needed someone to impart all this knowledge to, since she wasn't required to write papers or take tests.

Their mothers might have been very different people who had a strange dislike for each other, but they seemed to agree that little girls should not be made to conform to anything that did not ebb and flow like the tide: their minds, at the very least, should run rampant along the beach.

It helped that the mobile-library van drove from Seattle once a month, bringing books to all the stray houses along the coast. The librarian often brought biology textbooks for Jane and once even surprised her with some journals from the University of Washington because she knew how much Jane loved reading about scientific studies.

For Martha she brought fantasy or, once in a while, romance novels. Jane had tried to read one of the romances but rolled her eyes pretty quickly and went back to a battered copy of the *Farmers' Almanac*. Martha had rolled her eyes at that, especially since it dated to the early 1900s. 'Who cares about the weather in the past?' she'd asked.

'The past is important,' Jane had said. 'If it weren't, why would we care so much about who our father is?'

'Well, I'm sure he had nothing to do with a year of bad crops in 1922.'

Except for a jaunt into Vancouver to give birth to Jane herself, Jane's mama had never spoken of a life anywhere else, as if she had been born miraculously at the age of eighteen, holding a satchel and harbouring a gift for painting marine birds midflight.

The scattered sea-shaken houses on the cliffs overlooking the ocean had been built long ago, but they mirrored the people who came and went: reclusive and solitary, wind-beaten and up for grabs. Jane's mother had inherited hers from a widow whose husband had disappeared while fishing for halibut. When Mama (before she was called Mama, obviously) showed up with her satchel of art supplies, needing a home, the widow took it as a sign that she should hand over the house and move on. People here listened – mostly to the wind, but also to fate. The sea told them what they needed to know, and also when to stay and when to go.

Zoe as well seemed to have materialised out of the sand dunes on the beach, giving birth to Martha as if she'd sculpted her in the rye grass out of flotsam and jetsam, topped off with a head of flowing seaweed. (Martha and Zoe were so hairy they kept a screwdriver by the bathtub because the drain constantly needed to be cleaned.) Before she'd had Martha, Zoe had lived in almost every house on this beach, with one man or another, until one by one the men left – usually on a boat – and took nothing and everything with them.

The last one to leave had basically given Zoe his house, with its dark blue shutters that would not clasp, but according to Zoe's journal, he was not Martha's father.

Also according to Zoe's journal, there wasn't much to say about Martha's father.

Zoe and Mama were simply Zoe and Mama. Two women living according to the laws of nature, the sea, the sun, the moon, and their daughters.

For a while people came from all over to spend time on this particular stretch of beach, so even if not many people lived here, the girls didn't feel isolated or alone – at least, not when they were younger. The outside world came to them. Families with kids, couples without. They were from all different coasts and walks of life, of all different shapes and sizes. No one ever stayed long, but that was also the beauty of it: how transient people were.

One summer a guy from Slovenia came and sold ice

cream sandwiches out of an old abandoned bait and tackle shop. Nobody told him he couldn't, so he stayed longer than most. Jane and Martha went often to visit him, and he would give them free ice creams if they learned one Slovenian word a day. They kept trying to say thank you in Slovene, but it was impossible to make their tongues fit around the sharp edges of the words. Finally one day he said, 'Don't worry about it – I have a speech impediment in my own language. I'm not saying it the way they do back home either.'

He gave them each a chocolate-chip ice cream sandwich for their efforts.

'Do you think he could be our father?' Jane had whispered out of the corner of her mouth. He had dark hair, just like Martha. Jane was fair, with very fine, straight hair that pinged out of her braids, making her look a bit like a bedraggled hedgehog.

Martha surveyed the Slovenian ice cream guy and said, 'Nah, neither one of us has a speech impediment.' She had no idea what that was, but it was a big word, so if they'd had one, they would have known.

They were ten at the time. Jane was the one who had the Webster's dictionary, another gift from the travelling librarian, so she looked it up and confirmed that Martha was right: he probably wasn't their father.

'So, get this,' Martha said, flopping herself down on Jane's couch, making dust particles fly into the air.

'Oops. Sorry, Huckleberry.'

Jane's dog sniffed close to Martha, smelled her breath, then backed away suspiciously.

Jane laughed. 'What kind of toothpaste is Zoe making now?'

'Oh. Absinthe,' Martha said distractedly.

Jane had tried Zoe's toothpaste once, but it tasted like bird poop.

'Zoe's diary talks about how a guy built her an outhouse before he left,' said Martha.

'An outhouse?'

'Yeah, his last great token of love.'

'Wouldn't you have been considered a last great token of love, if he was your father? I mean, before an outhouse?'

Martha seemed not to have heard her.

Jane wondered then – and secretly not for the first time – if she and Martha could really have the same father. She knew her mother would not view an outhouse as a token of love.

Martha had started to worry Jane. She seemed restless and edgy, and a few steps ahead, as if she was already moving on from the only life they'd ever known.

And suddenly she was interested in outhouses? There were a few forgotten ones, tilting precariously along the bluffs, but the girls usually steered clear of them, for obvious reasons.

'You're on your own for this one,' Jane said. 'Not my thing. Not anyone's thing, actually.'

The last person who had used the abandoned outhouses had been the Slovenian ice cream man.

'Don't you want to know?' Martha asked. 'Maybe he carved his name in the wall or something.'

So Jane begrudgingly trudged along behind Martha to the slanted building punctuating the hillside. There had been no directions in Zoe's diary, and there were four other outhouses in various locations, but Jane didn't point this out because she hoped they were only going to check out the one that Martha had her sights on and then go eat the picnic lunch they'd brought along. It was so old it didn't even smell bad anymore. There were mouse turds along the wooden seat, and the blue Styrofoam was chewed all around the hole. An old licence plate from Washington state dangled precariously by one nail. The date said 1980: fifteen years ago.

'What if that was his?' Martha whispered as if they were in church, not a literal shit hole.

Both girls had been born in 1981, a few months apart. Of course their mothers couldn't be friends, just do the math! Something live scurried around down in the hole, and Huckleberry barked like a maniac.

'Can we go, please?' Jane said.

'I spend hours with you and your stupid molluscs,' Martha said, which was true.

'Okay, but what else is there to see?'

Martha shrugged. 'Yeah, you're right. Let's go have a picnic.'

It was a beautiful day, but clouds were hugging the far horizon, and the girls knew they needed to get to the other side of the beach, where, if the wind changed direction and it did rain, they'd just barely be out of reach of it.

Huckleberry got there first, spinning in circles and kicking up sand until the girls shooed him off so they could spread out their blanket and unpack their food: liverwurst sandwiches from Mama, barbecued tempeh from Zoe.

'If you write the word "love" on your water bottle, it makes the water taste better,' Martha told Jane as they sat hidden from view, out of the wind, sipping carefully because sand had crusted the rims of their bottles.

'You mean I won't notice the sand between my teeth if the bottle says "love"?' Jane asked.

Martha laughed. 'You're so funny, Jane. But yes, it can even change the physical composition of the water.'

'What do you mean, I'm so funny?'

'I just mean, you know, provincial.'

She said it as if she'd just looked it up and had been waiting for the right moment to use it. Which she probably had.

Martha also cleared her throat and announced, 'I'm going to remake myself into a totally different person.'

'Like who?' Jane asked, her mouth full of liverwurst.

'I don't know. Maybe a hippie.'

'Technically, I think you already are one,' said Jane, pointing at the tempeh sandwich.

'Okay, maybe not a hippie. I just want a chance to start over somewhere and be a whole new person. I think I'm ready to be in a bigger place. And I'm dying to have sex.'

Jane felt her face grow hot. So that was what Martha meant by provincial.

'God, Jane, see what I mean? You can't even talk about sex, which is the most natural thing in the world.'

If it was the most natural thing in the world, why did both their mothers act as though they'd all just washed up here at high tide?

But Zoe talked to Martha all the time about her body and the weird things it was doing, while Mama, of course, did not talk to Jane. And in this instance, Jane was relieved. But it was the first thing that had come between her and Martha, and it wasn't like she could just go hang out with other girls who were late bloomers like herself. Jane hadn't even gotten one zit yet. Martha had zits and armpit hair and boobs that had basically popped out of her chest one night while she slept.

Martha had been begging Zoe for ages to take her

to Vancouver to buy a bra, but of course, Zoe, who actually was a hippie, did not believe in bras.

'They cause cancer,' she said.

Jane thought Zoe was kidding. But she wasn't.

'All that underwire keeping your lymph nodes trapped. It's not natural. Everyone's waiting for the science to prove it, but by then, so many women will have died of cancer.'

Jane knew better than to tell Mama things Zoe said. Bras causing cancer would go into the same category as the time she'd mentioned Zoe had communicated telepathically with a bag of chips.

'Someone needs to take that woman's wineglass away,' was all Mama had had to say about that.

Martha was still talking about remaking herself and Jane was busy tuning her out, when Huckleberry started barking his head off at something on the opposite side of where they were hidden, out of the weather. The clouds hadn't lied: rain was suddenly beating down everywhere, except in their secret spot. Jane looked out and saw two kids struggling to pack up their buckets and shovels, caught totally off guard by the pelting rain.

'We should help them,' said Jane, noticing that the girl was about their age. She figured Martha would want to try out being 'a totally new person' on this stranger. Sure enough, while Jane was still thinking this, Martha was already off, with Huckleberry on her heels.

The boy had gotten interested in something along the water's edge and wandered off, leaving his sister (if it was his sister) to fill their netted beach bag with all the loose toys by herself, her drenched hair falling in her eyes, slowing her down.

Suddenly, a scream wrenched the air. Jane thought maybe Martha had stepped on a piece of glass – that had happened more than once to both of them – but it wasn't a Martha scream. Jane noticed there were more people on the beach than she'd realised, all caught off guard by the beautiful day that had turned on a dime. A wave of soaking wet beachgoers began to move toward the boy, who was at the edge of the water staring into a rubber boot and screaming his head off.

But what Jane was most impressed by was the speed with which the boy's sister ran, as if her feet had wings. Not even Huckleberry could keep up with her, and he was faster than the arctic terns that spun and whipped in the wind, terrorising him.

When the girl reached her brother, she grabbed the boot out of his hands and covered his whole face with her body. One quick glance inside and she dropped the boot in the sand and dragged her brother backward, trying to get away from it.

As adults arrived, it was scooped up and quickly

hidden away, so Jane and Martha never got to see firsthand what had caused all the commotion. But word travelled quickly, and eventually the boot ended up in police custody. The thing that had caused all the screaming was a severed human foot.

After just a week of police tape and investigations and everyone being treated as if someone had done something sinister, Martha and Zoe – both of whom Jane loved as much as she loved her own mother – up and moved to Colorado. Just like that, Martha got her wish to remake herself somewhere else.

They packed up Zoe's diaries and nailed the blue shutters closed, locking up the old secrets and the bath drains full of hair. Jane gave Martha her Webster's dictionary; she figured Martha needed it more than she did. They drove off in a half-empty moving van because Zoe didn't believe in material things. But she also said she didn't believe in living in a place where random body parts just materialised and made everyone suddenly suspicious. It wasn't good karma.

Mama said that so many people were lost at sea, it was amazing body parts didn't wash up more often. She and Jane were staying put.

Now Martha wrote Jane letters about Zoe's gazebo made of colourful liquor bottles (Mama had snorted at this but said nothing more) and how weird it was to not hear the ocean, but she still talked about it because this new life she had created meant pretending she was from California.

Martha told Jane that California was much more interesting than being from what she called 'the tiniest little isthmus on the edge of the Washington/Canada border where nothing ever happens'.

'An isthmus would actually connect two pieces of land,' Jane had written back. 'I think you're using the wrong word.'

Martha hadn't mentioned it again. 'I talk about you all the time,' she said. 'I told someone that you're the one who gave me the gardenia perfume.'

When Martha wrote that the poor girls from Middle Earth, Colorado, didn't even know what to do with gardenia perfume, Jane tried being facetious.

'Oh my God, you poor thing, you have gone back to the 1940s.'

IT. WAS. A. JOKE.

Jane didn't want to be part of Martha's lies, as if she wasn't interesting enough for real. And she had never smelled or seen gardenia perfume in her life.

She tried to bring Martha back to reality. 'The jig is up. Has anyone figured out that you're not from California but actually from a tiny thumb (not an isthmus) that juts into the Pacific Ocean?'

But Jane missed her friend terribly, and after the whole rubber-boot incident, Martha was right about one thing: nothing ever did happen here anymore. No couples strolling in the sunset. No kids building sandcastles. No more geeky-looking birders with long-lensed cameras and birding scopes and incredibly unattractive cargo shorts. Pretty much nobody came to the beach anymore except the last few locals who were too tired to leave, like Jane and Mama.

Jane would have been happy even to talk about sex, if Martha would come back.

And then one day, Huckleberry was nosing around looking for a lost ball when he startled and ran back to Jane, howling his head off.

'What's up, silly boy? Did you stir up the blue heron's nest again? You know she doesn't like that.'

Deep in his throat, Huckleberry growled, then pawed the ground but wouldn't go farther.

'What is it?' Jane said again, stepping gingerly up to the dune, parting the long beach grass with her fingers.

Oh no, she thought, seeing a pair of steel-toed boots lying side by side, noses up, as if they had bloomed out of the sand. She immediately thought of the other boot, the one with a human foot in it, and was slightly relieved that at least there were two of these and they were also attached to two long legs. It was a weird thing to notice, and she wished Martha were with her, especially when she realised that this was a whole person, intact but not looking very well.

He was probably a few years older than Jane, and his breathing was very, very shallow.

'Huckleberry, go get Mama!' Jane yelled, pointing to the house. But the dog just looked at her and cocked his head one way and then the other.

Jane took off as fast as she could, but she knew she was not the girl who had run like lightning when her brother had screamed. Jane did the best she could, her mind working faster than her legs, replaying the images in her head: salt-crusted leather boots, wet faded jeans, messy bowl-cut hair surrounding a pale face. Much too pale, actually. Ashes from a fire. An old tin can. Clamshells scattered nearby.

God, why do you always have to notice molluscs, even in an emergency? Martha was gone, but Jane could still hear her voice.

It took a concerted effort on the part of the few people still left to get the boy into a bed, warm him up, figure out who he was and how he'd gotten here. This last bit was going to be the most difficult, because even he wouldn't be able to tell them.

His licence said that his name was Conrad James, he was from Granville, Colorado, and he was nineteen years old. That was a real cowboy-sounding name, Jane thought, scanning the atlas she'd gotten from the mobile library. Granville was only about thirty miles from Pigeon Creek, where Martha now lived.

Seeing those towns on the map so close together reminded Jane of all the ways she and Martha had forever tried to make their lives intersect. Except that this boy landing where he did really was just a coincidence.

Conrad had planned to visit an uncle in Canada, one he barely knew but who he'd heard of often. His uncle had a PhD in physics, fixed up vintage cars, and lived with a man. Conrad had wanted to ask his advice: Was it really possible to live in this world and love whoever you wanted?

But he hadn't made it to Canada, because the beach had drawn him in, its beauty and mystery and the cacophony of waves hitting the rocks. And now Conrad had no idea that he even had an uncle. All of it was gone, just like that. He was a completely blank slate.

The last thing he'd done was dig a few razor clams, make a small fire, and cook them in an old tin can filled with salt water. He was from landlocked Colorado, nowhere near the ocean, so he did not know that digging and eating clams was only done in months containing an 'R'. As Martha's mother used to say, *You don't know what you don't know.*

But now he also didn't know things he had known. How he'd angrily stormed out of a church sacristy after seeing a priest touch an altar boy who was barely ten years old. He would not remember wondering if he should have told someone – the boy's mother? Most of all, he had no memory that that same priest had made him feel so much shame about a confessed kiss.

Sadly, that kiss, one of the most beautiful things Conrad had experienced in his life up to that point, would also be forgotten.

Jane knew none of these things about him either as she watched him sleeping in her bed, a warm washcloth on his forehead. But when he finally woke up and had no idea who he was or where he'd come from, she knew that her beloved bivalve molluscs were at the scene of the crime.

She found all of her old *Farmers' Almanac*s and the scientific journals that the librarian had brought her over the years. She remembered reading about a toxic substance called domoic acid that was thought to infect shellfish. Scientists were studying cases of people who had actually suffered amnesia after eating clams or mussels or even oysters contaminated by algae blooms. It had popped up a few times in these papers; there had even been outbreaks of amnesic shellfish poisoning on Prince Edward Island.

Of course, she couldn't test for it, but when the paramedics arrived she handed them a bag full of clamshells that had been on the ground near where she'd found him and told them her theory.

'Some people never recover, and others live their lives remembering only things that happened after they ate the shellfish; still others forget everything, even new things, over and over again. It's a matter of time, how it plays out long-term. Everyone is different. But he does have many of the symptoms.'

She couldn't believe how intently they listened to her, as if she were a real scientist.

They promised to send out health officials the next day to test live clams so that nobody else got sick. One of the paramedics smiled and said, 'You've just saved us hours of work trying to nail this down. At least now we have a place to start. Thank you.'

They had his ID and said they'd get in touch with his family, leaving Jane feeling like a real marine biologist and also sadder than she'd been in ages. She loved this beach, but maybe Zoe was right about its karma. And maybe there was a reason that the sea-shaken houses kept changing hands. Also, selfishly, she wished Martha could have seen firsthand that all those years of Jane studying bivalves had actually done some good.

As the ambulance pulled away, Jane walked behind it for a while, watching the lights blink and then fade out of sight. She fingered the postcard she'd found in Conrad's pants pocket when she'd taken his clothes to be washed. It was addressed to someone named

Ben, also in Granville, Colorado. It was a picture of a brilliant sunset and a view of the ocean. It could have been from anywhere, even California.

She'd read it a few times and felt an invisible hand twisting her stomach like wringing out a wet sock as she slid the postcard into her jacket before anyone else could see it.

It was the same feeling she'd had whenever Martha read her Zoe's diaries.

She knew secrets were meant to stay secret, but if he didn't remember anything or anyone, maybe she could help him connect with this part of his past, even if it was just a tiny gesture. She didn't know that Conrad had never planned to mail that postcard, because once again, *You don't know what you don't know.*

So Jane dropped the card into the weathered red metal mailbox covered in bird poop. Then she thought about Zoe's awful toothpaste all the way back to her house.

She also thought about secrets and memories.

Her mother was waiting with lavender tea, looking at Jane with questioning eyes, almost the way Zoe would have if she'd been around. Finding a boy with no past lying on the beach, well, Zoe wouldn't have been surprised by that and would have expounded on karma sticking its gnarled little fingers into everything once again.

But Mama just stuck to the facts as she poured boiling water into their cups.

'Pretty impressive for a girl who taught herself everything there is to know about molluscs,' she said. 'I'm really proud of you.'

Jane dunked her tea ball a few times and then passed it over for her mom to use.

'I was thinking maybe I have a future in marine biology after all. Maybe Martha isn't the only one with a life somewhere else.'

Mama smiled a sad smile and said she thought it was a brilliant idea.

Jane thought about Conrad washing up on the beach. It fitted with her mother's unspoken theory that the rising and falling tide pretty much decided all of their fates. She had little to lose anymore by asking direct questions, so she pushed her luck one last time.

'So, we didn't have the same father?'

'For someone who is practically a genius when it comes to bivalves, you certainly let Martha fill your head with strange ideas. Why on earth did you girls think that?'

'Because you and Zoe couldn't stand each other. We thought it was a lifelong quarrel over ... him. Whoever he was.'

'Jane, the woman talks to potato chips.'

'Well, now that you say it like that ...'

They both laughed, but then Mama reached over and held Jane's hands tightly in her own.

'Your father didn't even know about you. I just didn't think it was fair to make you think he might come looking.'

Jane had already figured this out, but she also wondered if it was her mother who wished he'd come looking. Why else would she insist on staying in this place when almost everyone else moved on? Mama did not believe in karma and her fingers were not gnarled, but they were warm, and holding them made Jane feel hopeful for both of them.

She thought again of a stranger named Conrad heading to a hospital all alone in an ambulance, with no idea who he was. At least he wasn't in a coma, which was another symptom of amnesic shellfish poisoning.

Maybe this Ben person was someone who would come looking for Conrad, once he got the postcard.

All of this hope had emboldened her.

'Can I go visit Martha and Zoe in Colorado?'

Mama stared at her hard for a couple seconds. Jane squirmed, unable to read her expression.

Had Mama hoped Zoe was out of her life for good?

Her mother stood up and left the table.

Jane thought she might cry. She had known better than to press Mama like that.

In the next room she heard a dresser drawer open

and then screech shut again. It was the heavy junk drawer, where she and Martha stashed anything interesting they found. She knew every broken shell in it, every odd-shaped rock, every piece of mottled beach glass. Their entire lives were there in the space of one sandy bureau drawer. Jane hadn't opened it since Martha left. Mama knew she wouldn't, not without her best friend to share it with.

It was a perfect hiding place.

A few seconds later she was back and sliding a bus ticket across the table toward Jane.

'It was supposed to be a surprise,' she said. 'Of course you should go visit Martha.'

Parking-lot Flowers

Ben had picked up the hitchhiker on the edge of town before he'd realised how young she was. Maybe fifteen, probably a runaway, and he really didn't need that. He so did not need that.

He'd finally gotten himself going, nudging his rusty Mustang out of town as if it were a reluctant horse by the same name. It was a feat that had required so much energy that picking up *anyone* could only be attributed to an exhausted lapse in judgement.

But how many times had he stood on the side of the road with his thumb out, in freezing rain, hoping against hope for a ride? *It's called 'empathy'*, he told himself. *The ability to put yourself in someone else's shoes.*

Hers weren't shoes; they were leather boots with back zips, and inside one of them, she'd slid a switchblade, nestled between her calf and a long woollen sock. He didn't know she had it, and she didn't know she wouldn't need it with him, but that's the beauty of strangers, all the things we cannot know.

He stereotyped her as a sullen, introverted runaway,

mainly because of the greasy hair hanging out of her purple hoodie.

Beware of stereotypes, he reminded himself, thinking of how Conrad had been voted most eligible bachelor and how all the girls in town vied for his attention. It was so easy to make people believe what they wanted to believe. Until it wasn't.

The hitchhiker had an expensive backpack with one of those Nalgene water bottles that hippies and climbers used, but if he had to guess, she was not a hippie or a climber. He leaned across her to get aspirin out of the glove box, and she flinched as if he might touch her.

Ben was a 'nice guy', to the point of being boring – he'd been told – and even though he was starting to regret picking her up, he was not used to being flinched around.

'Are you okay?' he asked.

'I'm just a moth attracted to the flame,' she said. Then she stared blankly out the window.

Was that sarcasm?

He wanted to tell her how much of a cliché that was, but then he remembered sitting around the campfire – just a year ago – with Conrad and his older sister, Lula, and her friends from college. Everyone had been feeling carefree. He and Conrad were about to graduate from high school. There had been something thrilling about being with Conrad's sister and her friends, drinking beers and passing a joint, just a few miles from where he was driving now. He passed the turnoff to the grate and cattle fence with the broken chain that all the kids in town knew was a ruse. Beyond it was the trail that led through thick pine and juniper trees and then opened out to nothing and everything at the same time. Their secret, beautiful place.

If he closed his eyes he could almost smell the lingering pot and woodsmoke and that mysterious girl smell he could never quite understand. One of them even smelled weirdly like oranges.

Lula had brought three girlfriends home to Granville during their college break. All her friends had very white teeth and long hair that hung straight like curtains down along their ears. They talked about things he and Conrad never really thought about, mostly politics and how messed up the government was. They kept telling Ben and Conrad to start paying attention, to start getting involved, to think about protesting or they'd be sorry, man. They said *man* a lot; everything was *Yeah, man* and *I know, man*. And *Can you believe it, man?*

They couldn't be serious. Protest where? In front of the Piggly Wiggly? These girls obviously had no clue about Granville. But that seemed silly. Two of them were sisters from a town just thirty miles up the canyon, Pigeon Creek, and it ticked all the same small-town boxes Granville did.

But Lula and her friends seemed to think that by going to college they had cracked some mysterious code that people from small towns could never crack. Granville did not qualify as being in 'the real world'. Or maybe they just wanted to believe that.

When they laughed – even though nothing seemed all that funny – their white teeth stood out like miniature marshmallows lining dark caves inside their faces. He imagined pulling one out of the mouth of the girl closest to him, skewering it on the end of a sharpened willow and roasting it in the fire until it turned black.

It had to be the pot affecting him, because it was disturbing to think he could come up with that all on his own.

Conrad had slung a Coleman lantern up in a tree, and when Ben stood up he'd knocked his head on it. Everyone had laughed. He was always jostling and bumping into things, trying to navigate a world that was getting smaller and smaller around him, like Jack and the beanstalk, except that he *was* the beanstalk.

He was constantly teased about how long and lanky he was. Just getting up to take a piss and knocking the lantern might have caused a forest fire, which was not a joke. It was always fire season in the west, especially near Granville, which had been in a drought for the past decade.

He'd steadied the lantern and immediately noticed the moth. Somehow it had squeezed its furry wings inside the little glass doors, and it was licking the flames, either hungrily unaware of the danger or too much in love to care.

Whenever Ben smoked weed the world was slower, fuzzy around the edges, not unlike the moth's wings. Its eyeballs, however, were inky, like humungous poppy seeds, hypnotised by the heat that bounced off the tiny glass doors of the lantern, which looked warm and inviting. Ben would have squeezed inside himself too, if he could have managed it.

While everyone else had babbled on about how the world was going to hell in a hand basket (what did that even *mean*?), he had watched the little creature die. He was helpless to do anything else. It could have been him inside that lantern, drawn to all that dangerous orange heat.

Now, as he drove, he thought about the smoky wings and the slow lapping flame against the moth's body. If only he'd paid more attention.

He wondered if the moth had actually been a warning: Be wary of too much beauty and light.

He had kissed Conrad that same night, admitting that he'd wanted to for years. And Conrad had kissed him back. But now Conrad was gone and Ben could not see the road because his eyes were getting blurry.

He swerved the Mustang onto a pullout near the river, where it curved dangerously around a bend and then dropped into a steep ravine.

'I need some air,' he said, slamming the door and leaving the girl staring openmouthed at him as he bolted, scattering scree down toward the river's edge with his long legs.

He could feel her eyes on him as he squatted next to an eddy where the river formed a little bowl. He crouched near the small pool, but to reach it he still had to bend again, like folding a towel in thirds the way his mother did.

Over and over again he scooped the icy water into his cupped hands and then splashed it on his face.

Watching from the car, the girl shivered and fingered her knife, opening and closing it as if in a trance, running her hand lightly over the blade.

He was sitting on a rock when she finally got out and slowly walked toward him. He wasn't sure if he was scared of her or if it was the other way around. He was watching a small animal with funny ears scurry across a fallen tree and cross over to a patch of something pink blooming on the opposite bank.

It stood up when she got close and wrinkled its nose in the air so its whiskers waggled. Its tiny paws were folded in front of it, as if in prayer, but as she got near, it let out an earsplitting shriek.

'Marmots are so cute,' she said, her hands over her ears, 'but he's loud, isn't he? . . . Or she?'

She looked terrified, as if she hadn't meant to say the word 'cute'. Ben felt that familiar sensation he got, even around people he didn't know. Always the pleaser, sensing everyone's moods and needing to make people feel comfortable.

Trying too hard was how Conrad described it.

'That's a pika,' he said, tapping a stick against his leg, 'not a marmot.'

'Oh. What's the difference?'

Seriously? They were going to pretend to care about pikas versus marmots?

'Um, well, pikas look more like little rabbits, but no tail, and they're rounder and fuzzier.'

It was the longest sentence he'd uttered since he'd picked her up.

'Marmots don't have that high-pitched alarm call like pikas do,' he went on. 'And they hibernate for almost seven months in their dens, all curled up with each other, their hearts beating once every hour or so . . .' He trailed off when his voice started to sound irritating in his own ears, too know-it-all.

'I wouldn't mind sleeping for a few months,' she said.

The circles around her eyes gave the impression that

she'd been asleep for decades. He'd seen zombies in movies that looked better than she did.

'Well, there's a dark side in the marmot world,' he said, thinking of beauty and light, not wanting to sound too much like a pleaser. 'If the teenage girl marmots come back to the den pregnant, after doing whatever they do with the boy marmots, the mothers will punch them with their fists until they abort. They just don't have room for extra bodies all winter.'

The girl looked at him with an unreadable expression.

'I'm sorry. That was blunt,' he said, taking her blank face for horror. 'It's not really about morality in the animal kingdom.'

He wondered if she was one of those animal-rights-type people as she turned her back on him.

She crumpled like a paper bag in the wind, and he thought maybe she was crying or perhaps even sick.

Ben looked away, giving her the only privacy he could, that of not watching. But after a few minutes he couldn't stand it.

He went over and stood in the shallow pool next to her, shaking out a handkerchief and soaking it in the clear, cold stream. He wrung it out and handed it to her.

When she finally turned around he realised she was laughing. Maniacal, sleep-deprived laughter that looked painful. She took the handkerchief and buried her face in it, her shoulders shaking uncontrollably.

What the hell? He turned abruptly back to the car.

By the time she'd dragged herself up the bank, she was completely composed, once again the sullen introvert he'd picked up.

'How far are you going?' he asked.

She had pulled the hoodie strings so tight around her face she looked like a lumpy purple Mr Potato Head, her lips pursed out like a fish.

'I'm going to hell. Straight to hell,' she whispered in a sing-songy cadence. She was badly in need of ChapStick.

'How about I let you out in Baker?' he said.

'Fine. And don't worry, I couldn't care less about morality in the animal kingdom.'

Baker was forty miles away, which seemed like a long time to have to sit next to her.

The only radio station he could get was run out of the basement of mountain man Coyote Jones. It was definitely not FCC legal, but somehow Jones managed to stay on the air, fuzzy reception in and out of the local towns scattered all the way to the Wyoming and Nebraska borders.

Ben kept it on, because even static inside the Mustang was more comforting than being totally alone with a lunatic, although there were rumours about the sanity of Coyote Jones as well. There's a difference between a familiar lunatic and one you know nothing about. As he'd often heard his mother say, 'The people here are crazy, but they're *our* kind of crazy.'

Ben was fairly certain that 'our kind of crazy' did not include being gay. Not in 1995 in Granville, Colorado, anyway. Maybe in some far-off city like Los Angeles or New York, where there were enough people that you could slide between hundreds of bodies and be virtually unnoticed, but not here, in the middle of nowhere. There was no anonymity in a small town. Especially if you stood out at all.

No, he should never have kissed Conrad. And probably Conrad wished he had never kissed him back.

'Well, folks, we've got a hot spot burning just south of Granville. Looks like it's picked up some traction on the western ridge, where all that fuel has been waiting to be kissed by some red-hot love.'

Coyote Jones often used these kinds of analogies to describe the weather, and usually people thought it was funny. But just now, with a stranger in the car and him thinking about kissing Conrad, Ben didn't find it humorous. He rolled down his window to get a little air.

At least the fire would be heading in the other direction if Coyote Jones had his information straight, which he almost always did.

'This one just looks like good old-fashioned arson – a dumpster fire that got a little out of control.'

The radio abruptly turned to static.

'He'll be back around the next corner,' said Ben, as if she might be worried.

'That guy's voice creeps me out anyway.' Her face looked even paler than before.

The stereo speakers hissed and crackled like a bowl of Rice Krispies.

'People trust him,' Ben said quietly. 'Coyote Jones, I mean.'

'I have good instincts,' she said. 'The guy sounds like a nutcase.'

'You aren't from around here, are you?'

She wouldn't be saying this if she was.

'Nope,' she said.

'So who were you visiting?'

'You wouldn't know them.'

'Obviously you don't know Granville. Everyone knows everyone.'

'Are you trying to make friends suddenly?' she asked, in the unfriendliest tone ever.

Definitely not, he thought, pressing a little harder on the gas.

Ben had tried to talk to Conrad at Mass the Sunday after the kiss, but Conrad wouldn't even look at him. He was coming out of the room where they kept the chalices and where the altar boys prepared the wine and hosts for Communion. Conrad was the head acolyte, the one who trained the younger altar boys about everything from what to wear (black pants, dress shoes) to how to stand (hands together, fingers straight) and sit (hands on knees). Ben thought the whole thing was ridiculous, but it was also something he loved about Conrad – the way he said church made him feel connected to something outside himself. Ben understood that, but it was Conrad who made him feel that way, not God.

Ben hadn't wanted to do anything to jeopardise Conrad's relationship with God; he had just wanted to talk. So he'd gone early, knowing that on that day the priest was hearing confessions. He thought that if Conrad didn't go to confession, Ben wouldn't have to wonder if he was regretting the kiss or if he felt guilty about it. Okay, maybe it was too much like spying, but he'd needed to know.

From the back of the church, watching Conrad enter the confessional was like being punched in the heart. Of course Ben should have left, given him privacy, but instead he inched closer, leaning his head against the mahogany door, breathing in the paraffin smell of candles and guilt. He heard Conrad's confession, whispered quietly, begging for forgiveness. The priest said something about the sins of the flesh, and to go forward and sin no more. Ben was instantly pissed off, but he managed to get outside before Conrad saw him. What a load of bullshit. He wanted to pick up a rock and throw it through one of the stained-glass windows.

He would not let this go. He was going to talk to Conrad directly.

He went back inside to the small room where the altar boys prepared for Mass, hoping to catch Conrad as he put away the incense and the chalice of Communion wine. The priest in the doorway was not Father Doyle but someone new. Ben had never seen this priest, who was dishevelled and had strands of grey hair combed sideways across his scalp. His furrowed bushy brows were watching someone leave hastily through the wide front doors of the building.

Behind the priest, in the small room, a young altar boy holding the chalice was staring out at Ben like a deer in the headlights.

'Are you all right?' Ben asked, stepping closer to peer inside.

Both the boy and the priest flinched at the sound of Ben's voice.

'What's your name?' Ben asked him.

'Michael,' said the boy, his voice barely audible.

The priest tried to shut the door, but Ben held his hand against it. 'You look terrified, Michael,' he said. 'Are you okay?'

'I need to go find my mom.'

Ben pushed his hand harder against the door, and the priest stumbled backward, caught off balance on the other side. Michael dropped the chalice with a clang and hurried past. He looked barely ten years old.

'Everything okay?' Ben asked the priest, who had recovered his footing and was again pushing the door closed.

'Why wouldn't it be?' he said, bolting it from the inside.

There was something really strange about that priest. Nobody ever stormed away from Father Doyle, or looked scared like that altar boy had looked. The thought of Michael's big brown eyes continued to haunt Ben. He had tried for over a week afterward to reach Conrad but had no luck – Conrad didn't take his calls and wasn't home when Ben dropped by. Finally Lula had come to the door to say that Conrad had left town. He hadn't even said goodbye.

Two weeks later Ben received a postcard with a poem that explained nothing. It read like a suicide note.

> Green shoes thrown carelessly on a dry,
> wooden porch,
> Filterless Camel cigarettes
> And torn tablecloths holding half-
> empty beer bottles.

You're too beautiful for any of this.
And because I cannot apologise enough,
I plant flowers in old leather boots.
And fear the root-bound violet
Will die before morning.

Ben knew Conrad had an uncle in Canada, and the postmark on the card was from a place very close to the border. Was it a cry for help? Apologise for what? The kiss? For leaving? Was Ben the root-bound violet or was that Conrad?

He could not shake the feeling that Conrad wouldn't have sent it if he didn't want Ben to come looking for him.

Now he really wished he could read the poem one more time, scan it for some missing clue, but it was in the glove box and he wasn't going to reach across his passenger again. Coyote Jones's voice returned, making them both jump as if he'd popped into the backseat. Ben saw the girl's hand move to the top of her boot. She caught him looking and then pretended to be massaging her leg. She was hiding something, but Ben hoped she'd be out of his car soon and he told himself he didn't care. He was tired of secrets.

It was dusk, and the streetlights in Baker were just blinking on when they pulled off the interstate.

'You'll be okay?' Ben asked. The Texaco beckoned

like a terrified animal crouched in the shadows. Someone had shot at the sign, and the 'X' was the only light that still worked – sort of – if blinking intermittently counted as working.

She opened the door before he'd even slowed all the way down at the pump, mumbling something that sounded like 'bathroom key'. The way she bolted made him think again of the altar boy, running off in search of his mother.

Ben filled the tank, went inside, and paid the woman behind the counter. She popped her gum and blew a bubble right in Ben's face, then laughed. She had wobbly ears, made even more wobbly by the feather earrings that hung clear down to her shoulders. The nest on top of her head looked like it was held together by a whole can of hair spray, as if she was working hard on a theme. Even her eyeshadow was robin's-egg blue.

'Git in a fight with yer friend?'

'Excuse me?'

'Yer girlfriend. She scooted out the back. Seemed like she was in a real hurry, stole my bathroom key.'

Outside, Ben checked the doors to the bathrooms, but they were locked.

He walked around the building, but all he saw were open garbage cans billowing trash everywhere and crows having a smelly feast. There was no sign of the girl. On the other side of the interstate was a shabby-looking motel. Its sign was also shot out, as if Ben had arrived just after neon hunting season. If she had left, she probably didn't want him to go after her.

Well, good riddance, he thought. But he had reservations about just leaving without knowing where she'd gone. Why couldn't she have thanked him and said goodbye like a normal person?

Because everyone left him like this, he realised. Stranded in the dark on the side of the road.

Conrad used to tease Ben for caring too much about things that weren't his problem: birds that flew into windows, returning lost gloves to their owners, and now the sudden disappearance of a girl with greasy hair and zombie eyes who he never should have picked up in the first place.

He pretended not to see the woman with her face pressed against the window of the Texaco, smudging the glass with her breath. It was hard not to miss the feather earrings being blown by the fan behind her head, as if trapped birds were banging their wings against the windowpane.

He pulled back onto the interstate, pointing the Mustang west, determined to put more distance between himself and Granville.

'But you don't even know where you're going,' his mother had said when he'd told her he was leaving.

'The postmark was in Washington, just below

Vancouver, BC,' said Ben. 'I'll call you when I get there.'

'That's a pretty big place – I'm sure Conrad isn't expecting you to chase him down. You should wait in case he comes back.'

'Well, he doesn't get to weigh in, now, does he? He didn't ask me if *he* could leave.'

'Honey . . .'

But Ben hadn't heard what came after, because he'd been stomping up to his room and then had slammed the door. He didn't usually stomp. Or slam. But nothing made sense anymore. He was terrified that Conrad was dead, so of course driving to the place that had swallowed him up was the only thing Ben could think of doing. Which meant maybe he hadn't totally lost hope?

Now it was just him and Coyote Jones alone on I-87. He saw signs for the Pawnee National Grasslands and couldn't tell if he actually smelled wildfire smoke or if Coyote Jones's description just made him imagine that he could. The fire had grown and was threatening towns to the east of Granville. Coyote Jones said residents in neighbouring towns should be prepared to evacuate quickly if the order was given.

Everyone trusted Coyote Jones; his voice was as much a part of the landscape in this area as the dry sage and noxious purple loosestrife that grew along the trails and streams. Nobody Ben knew had ever even seen him, but in Ben's mind Coyote Jones had one of those silky, waxen moustaches that curlicued at the corners of his mouth. Obviously he chain-smoked and probably shaved his head (to enhance his moustache).

Funny how some guy with an illegal radio station was more trusted than anyone from the Forest Service or the state. It was always this way. If Coyote Jones said there would be a winter storm, people stocked up on canned food and batteries, but if the state put out a weather advisory, nobody even bothered to bring their horses in from the fields.

Around here people trusted their own, not outsiders, no matter how many degrees they had in natural resource management. In fact, the more diplomas someone waved around, the more suspicious the locals became.

Ben imagined the scene in Granville and all the neighbouring towns within earshot of Coyote Jones's station, people hovering near their radios, waiting for instructions. Even though it did sound like the fire was heading east, away from town, he decided to take the next exit and call his mom, just to check in.

And that was when he saw it: the girl's fancy backpack shoved under the passenger seat. Not like something that had been accidentally left behind, but purposefully stashed. He opened it and found a book of matches with 'Granville' written on the inside cover, a piece of torn white fabric, and a few gum wrappers.

'Ben, please come home,' said his mother through the phone line that smelled like a campfire. He imagined each word she spoke hanging in the air, charred by smoke and secrets.

'Mom, I need to find Conrad. I think something terrible has happened to him.'

He cried messy tears, as if he were five years old again and had just fallen off his bike.

'Lula called. Conrad was in a hospital on the coast; his dad went out there to get him. She was hoping you'd be here when he got back.'

'Wait. What? Is he okay?' He held his breath.

'Well, that's why Lula called. He's okay, except ... he can't remember anything. Not even his name. Lula thinks maybe seeing you will help.'

'Why did he have to leave without telling me what was going on?' Now he was crying so hard he could barely hear what she was saying. Conrad was alive.

'There are some things in life that people have a hard time even telling themselves.'

He thought about the hitchhiker, her backpack, whatever it was she was hiding. If this pack wasn't stolen, then her name might be Delia – which was what was written inside in black marker – but he doubted she'd wanted anyone to know that.

He wondered if Conrad would remember their kiss now. Or even Ben himself. Or why he'd left in the first place. So many secrets.

'I'll be there in a few hours.'

And if Conrad didn't remember him, well, they had time. They'd just have to start over, and that wasn't the worst thing that could have happened. Ben wouldn't let him get away again.

Conrad is alive.

Conrad is alive.

He slid down the wall of the phone booth and looked at the forgotten bits of people's lives lying on the ground near his feet. Cigarette butts, a syringe, the stub of a bus ticket to Boise. A piece of blue chewing gum with teeth marks still in it. The rusty hinges of the phone booth kept the door from closing all the way, and just outside, in the pavement, one single purplish-blue flower was growing straight out of the cement. A pansy or a petunia or something else, he wasn't sure. Conrad was the one who knew the names of flowers, not Ben.

'You shouldn't be here,' he said out loud to the little parking-lot flower. 'You're too beautiful for any of this.'

The Right Kind of People

By the time Delia was sixteen she had a gum-wrapper chain that was forty feet long.

One of her many babysitters had shown her how to make it when she was five. Probably Michelle, since she was the one Delia remembered best; she smelled minty and was always at the ready with a piece of chewing gum.

'Only use the outside wrapper with the colourful designs. The foil won't work and isn't as pretty,' Michelle had told her, sliding the stick of gum from its wrapper, removing the foil, and popping it into her mouth. Then she opened the wrapper wide, folded it in half lengthwise, licked it to crease it, and split the two halves apart. The first one she folded in half again, then again, until it was skinny as could be, and then she folded it in half the other direction. She took one end and folded it yet again, to meet in the middle, then did the same to the other side. Michelle's flying fingers boggled Delia's mind, but she persisted and made her smaller, clumsier fingers mimic Michelle's over and over again, ruining heaps of wrappers before she got it right. Once it stuck, it stuck.

The tiny finished product had a little V shape that you could pretend was a mouth. And then you folded the other half of the wrapper and it fitted into the first V's mouth, and then the next one fitted into that one's mouth, et cetera, et cetera, and it just kept going. 'You could go forever if you wanted to,' said Michelle. 'I wish I'd started when I was your age, but now I'm too busy, you know, being a teenager and everything.'

Delia did not know what that meant, 'being a teenager and everything'. But she wanted a very long gum chain, so she decided to get cracking before anything having to do with being a teenager crept up on her. (Michelle had said it as if it was something you got even if you didn't want it, like the chicken pox.)

Whenever Delia went to the store she would scan the candy aisle for a brand of gum with a colour she didn't have yet and beg her parents to buy it. She had a lot of green Wrigley's Spearmint wrappers, and the yellow ones too, called Juicy Fruit. She loved the chequered gum that tasted like oranges and the black jack wrapper, but she hated the spicy liquorice taste of that gum, so she gave it to her brother. She kept all her wrappers in an old tobacco box. The gum she stashed in a paper sack, stripped of everything but their foil undies – this made her giggle like mad, the image of gum wearing *undies* – until she had no idea which flavour was which. She got really tired of chewing gum, and the sticks piled up in the paper bag.

Her parents never said no to gum, because they had a lot of money and she could have asked for anything, like another pair of cowboy boots or another fringy leather jacket (she had six). That was the thing about being the child of a rich Wyoming rancher: you could have whatever you wanted. So packs and packs of chewing gum was nothing at all.

The only rule was that she could not fold gum wrappers in church. Her parents were very Catholic. They gave a lot of money to the church, and her family had their own pew that they sat in every Sunday, in the very front row on the left side of the altar, where everyone could see them. Because of this, Delia and her brother had to look shinier than their friends, and they had to sit up straighter and fidget less than anyone else.

One whole stained-glass window was also paid for by her father's ranch: the seventh station of the cross, Jesus falls a second time. Her mother gave her a rosary to stop her fingers from pretending to fold and unfold invisible gum wrappers while she sat in the pew staring up at the image of Christ shouldering the cross. Behind him, his disciples looked worried, while other onlookers appeared to be jeering. She wished her daddy had left the soldier out of it, the one who was poking

Jesus with a spear, trying to make him stand up, but her daddy said it didn't work that way: 'Some things you cannot change, not even with money.'

At home there were barely any rules at all because home wasn't a place where they had to impress strangers. Delia and her brother could do almost anything they wanted, and there was a lot of laughing and running and sliding down the wide bannisters. There were ranch hands to joke with, and the general chaos of a house that has its own cook and maids who were constantly saying things like 'I just mopped; go the other way around in those muddy boots.' There were inside dogs and outside dogs but only ever outside cats – because her brother was allergic – but they were needed to chase mice in the barn. Delia loved the cats and would go outside to snuggle them, but they weren't used to being snuggled, and once she'd gotten a long scratch down her arm that got infected. She'd had to get a special shot because of it.

'Cat scratch fever,' said her brother. 'You're going to start drooling and then crawling around on all fours and your hair is going to fall out.'

Delia started to cry.

'I'm just kidding,' he said, because he hated it when Delia cried. 'Here, I got you some new red gum wrappers, what do you say? It's cinnamon flavour. I found it at that huge grocery store in Casper, when

Daddy took me with him last time. Please, Delia, stop crying.'

Delia's gum-wrapper chain was almost four feet long by the time she was seven. It was the same year she'd been given the important job of carrying the incense down the aisle during Easter services. Her brother was an altar boy already, holding the bucket so the priest could sprinkle holy water on the congregation, and they'd needed another set of hands. She could see the proud gleam in her mother's eye, and was extra careful to do it exactly right.

Delia loved church. She loved the fresh-cut flowers on the altar and the way the light played with the stained glass, making the colours splash like a rainbow across her brother's white robe. She loved the smell of incense, and that day, because of her job, she was bathed in it. She threw back her shoulders and stepped carefully, slowly swinging the censer back and forth, back and forth on its chain. She moved only her eyes to glance sideways at her mother when she got close to her family's pew. Delia knew she had been specially chosen to do this important thing, and the look on her mother's face told her that God thought so too. Or at the very least, everyone else in the church should be thinking so.

She felt like the holiest person in the world, walking serenely in front of her brother and the priest while the whole town watched.

The new nanny was told to wash Delia's hair twice that day because the first time it wasn't shiny enough to be seen from the very back pews. Her mother was keenly aware that that was where Lavinia Johnson would be sitting all alone, or with her eighty-five-year-old mother, whose eyesight wasn't very good. Delia had heard the ranch hands talking about Lavinia while they smoked outside the barn and she sat, unnoticed, in the hay with Tom Tom, the mouser.

'She's a beaut,' Hank had said, 'and now that her husband's bit it, she comes with a fair-sized wad.'

The other ranch hands had chortled and nudged Hank, while Delia wondered what it was Lavinia's husband had bitten. Or maybe she'd misheard and something had bitten him, like a rabid dog? (That really would make you crawl around and drool and act generally wild.) But either way – whether he'd bitten or been bitten – it clearly wasn't good, unless you were his wife, who was now rich with life insurance money. Delia didn't know what that was either, but every time her mother was on the phone gossiping with Delia's aunt – who'd followed the wrong guy (so it was said) and now worked in a twenty-four-hour diner in Colorado, which Delia's mother really lost sleep over – she lowered her voice a certain way specifically on those words, *life insurance money.*

Before Lavinia's husband died, the Johnsons had

lived simply, like everyone else in town, but now Lavinia and her mother had expensive coats and a new car, and they were moving to a bigger place with a lot of acreage, because she'd invested in a new technology called a wind turbine. Town was where people lived if they could only afford to rent. People who lived on ranches or had those funny-looking drills like hammers poking out of the ground that they leased to the oil companies, or now, like Lavinia, invested in wind farms, these were the people who came to Delia's parents' dinner parties.

The poor husband who'd bitten it had never been to one of the parties, because the Johnsons weren't *those kind of people* when he was alive.

On dinner party nights, Delia would sit in her room making her gum chain and notice who was coming and going outside her window. If someone was invited, they were what her mother called 'the right kind of person'. One night Delia had seen Lavinia emerge from a brand-new car with her mother. They both wore long evening gowns that also looked brand new. Hank had been scrubbed up, along with another ranch hand, and they were escorting guests from the cars to the front door. Delia giggled a little, seeing Hank with his hair plastered flat against his skull and no Stetson to hide it, so his head looked naked. He took Lavinia's mother's shaky old arm and led her up the steps, but his legs were bowed wide, and he mounted the stairs as if he were straddling an invisible horse.

'Too bad Lavinia's husband never got to come to a party,' Delia said to the new sitter, whose name she'd already forgotten. Her mother was tired of teenagers like Michelle not turning up when they were supposed to, so she'd hired someone much older tonight, someone with little hairs on her chin. Delia had learned from her mother how to make small talk and was hoping to impress this hairy lady, who also lived in town but was not fun like Michelle had been.

'I'm sure her husband didn't mind never being invited,' the woman said with an audible sniff. Her voice had a peppery sting to it that made Delia go quiet.

Didn't mind? she thought. The parties were everything. Her mother had not been raised in Wyoming but in Boston, so she knew a thing or two about how to throw a party. And she was determined to bring civility to her new home in the Rockies, even if it meant forcing her ranch hands into clothes that didn't smell like wet horses and manure and keeping constant vigilance over the dry red dirt incessantly carried in by boisterous winds and dogs and children.

Delia's mother was never more in her element than when she was throwing a party. The catering staff barely knew how to carry a tray of martinis without spilling – but they had better not! – while her mother could twirl holding hers above her head and not lose a single drop. Her hair was piled higher than anyone else's, her dresses were more sparkly, and her laugh was so high it bounced off the chandelier. Delia loved watching it all from the top of the staircase in her flannel pajamas and fuzzy slippers, with her gum wrappers next to her and her fingers folding and unfolding tiny Vs that she fitted together one inside the other, perfectly.

A lot of the money that swirled around them Delia's daddy got from breeding cows with his prize bull, Brutus. Delia used to laugh when Brutus would try to walk with his huge bulbous ball sack hanging down and his penis practically hitting the ground like a fifth leg. Her brother used to laugh like crazy when Delia said 'penis', especially at the breakfast table. The first time, he'd spluttered orange juice out his nose and her parents had looked shocked and then everyone laughed and she'd felt like the funniest person in the world. She was six.

But a year later, when she said that Father Lazaria had unzipped his pants in front of her and showed her his penis, they did not find this funny. (Although Delia had not been trying to make anyone laugh or spurt juice out of their nose anyway.)

Father Lazaria was a man of God, and a family friend. He often came to the house for dinner, and her parents had always smiled and nodded at her when he wanted her to sit on his lap during dessert. Under the table, where no one else could see, there was a bulge in the priest's lap that had made sitting there uncomfortable, but her mother scolded her when she tried to get down. Maybe, Delia had thought, priests had to wear robes during Mass because they didn't want everyone to know about their bulging crotches?

Delia was leery of getting very close to Father Lazaria once she'd experienced his uncomfortable lap, but she tried to be polite about it.

It had happened on Easter when she was just finishing her important job of carrying the incense back into the sacristy. She was allowed to go alone to return the censer to where it was stored, in what looked like a gilded birdcage. As she turned the key to open the little door and set the incense inside, she heard a click: the door was being bolted behind her. When she turned around, Father Lazaria had spread his arms wide and was lifting his robes, facing her with outstretched wings, like a huge purple phoenix sucking all the air out of the room.

Instantly, the smell of incense went from being something Delia loved to being something that made her gag. It caught in the back of her throat, and she thought she might throw up. Then he pulled his penis out of his fly and held it out to her in a way that could have been a joke, but not the kind of joke her father or brother ever played. Her gag reflex kicked in, and before she could stop herself, she really was vomiting. All over her shiny black shoes. He'd tucked himself away and looked disgustedly at her.

Her parents had given her the same look when she'd tried to tell them. She didn't know what she had done, but as she stumbled over words to describe what she'd seen, it became clear that no matter which words she chose, none of them were what her parents wanted to hear. Her mother informed her that what she said made no sense. Such things simply did not happen in their world.

But her parents didn't make her sit on his lap anymore when he came to dinner, and she wasn't allowed to carry the incense again. Her 'punishment' was that they kept her away from the poor priest so she couldn't tarnish his shiny image. Nothing else was said, but even her brother was different after that. He didn't tease her anymore, didn't try to make her laugh, and especially didn't make jokes about Brutus.

It happened so quickly and quietly that it would have been easy to think she was imagining it. She only knew that whatever had caused her family to stop laughing was her fault.

If everyone was going to treat her like this, she thought, it would have been better to just say nothing.

Her brother avoided her eyes, especially when

he went early to church to dress as an altar boy. She began to wonder if she'd really seen what she thought she'd seen.

When she was eight, she knelt across from Father Lazaria in the confessional box for the first time, just a thin mesh partition between them. Gratefully, she didn't have to see his face. But his breath filled the whole space: prunes soaked in spirits, a rancid old-man smell. She turned herself blue trying not to breathe it in, but she still felt covered in it. She had to make her First Confession in order to make her First Communion, and Delia still believed back then that the sacraments were holy. She'd desperately wanted to take Communion, because she thought the body of Christ would fix everything that was slipping out from under her eight-year-old feet. She was afraid that God had forgotten her, and even thinking that way made her feel like a terrible doubty person.

Father Lazaria had had to coax her to say the required words out loud: 'Bless me, Father, for I have sinned.' He had cut a small hole in the wall just above where she knelt and a curtain hung over it – apparently nobody else had noticed? – as soon as he heard her voice, his hand reached through the secret hole and slid itself between her legs. That first time she had screamed and jumped out of the confessional, but the look on her mother's face, as everyone kneeling and lighting candles had turned to stare, told her that she was again, somehow, the problem.

Why do you insist on behaving this way? said her mother's eyes.

After the not sitting on his lap at dinner, and the throwing up on her own shoes, Delia knew the drill. She decided the only thing to do was to stay one step ahead of him.

She became a tiny contortionist, fitting herself into all the different-sized boxes of expectations and disappointments that she now realised made up her family. In turn, they furrowed their brows and began to wonder if she was going mad (but only in the back of their minds, never out loud) as her obsession with fitting gum wrappers together grew more and more urgent.

Every time something happened with Father Monster (his name inside Delia's head), she made a black mark on her gum chain so that she would know how much time had passed by how many gum wrappers she'd folded. If she folded quickly, she could put more distance between herself and the unspeakable things: twelve feet. Fourteen feet. Sixteen and a half feet. Her childhood was measured in gum wrappers.

Delia and her brother drifted from their parents' orbit the way the earth tilts on its axis and the sun and moon never touch, except for the rare eclipse when they stare at each other face to face and the world goes black.

The catered dinner parties also grew old. Delia no longer found them entertaining, and she tried to block out her parents laughing uproariously over the sound of the martini shaker – At what? Who could say? – while the only thing she never got tired of was the soothing, meditative folding and fitting together of gum wrappers. The chain had grown to almost twenty feet by the time the dreaded 'being a teenager and everything' began to smack her in the face.

It had been years since her father had told her 'There are some things you cannot change, not even with money,' and yet, the gut-punching reality was that he was going to try anyway.

Delia was used to cold hard cash being shoved in her face, but she got even more if she looked like she was on the verge of asking a question or saying anything about anything. A hundred-dollar bill stuffed into the pocket of her boot-cut jeans was her father's idea of spending money.

For this reason, she wasn't just the nutty girl with a gum chain. She had plenty of so-called friends who were willing to be treated at the soda fountain or who invited her to go shopping in Casper because Delia was generous and could be counted on to make up the difference on a favourite sweater or jeans from

Hickson's Dry Goods. So what if the other girls whispered among themselves that she was 'overly quiet and a little strange'? (She could hear, you know.) She honestly didn't care. Not about the money or whether people wanted to be her friend. She was too busy keeping herself together. It reminded her of having an ingrown toenail, a thing that was constantly pressing into you, silently, painfully, although nobody else even knew it was there.

Her parents still expected her to go to church and receive Communion from Father Monster's shrivelled, stinky hand. They were firm believers that the host must come straight from the priest in order to be a true sacrament. She dreaded feeling his index finger skim her lip as he placed the white host on her shaky tongue. She tried to snatch her tongue back as quickly as possible, but his hairy knuckle might touch her face if she jerked, and she couldn't risk throwing up again, right there on the altar, while the line of communicants stretched behind her as long as a serpent's tail.

She imagined what they'd say, could hear their thoughts as a collective rattle in her head: *How dare she grimace at receiving the body of Christ?*

Delia no longer wanted to be seen at all, let alone sitting in the front pew. Anyone who looked might have thought she was still the chosen, holy child, head bowed, praying the rosary. But she had begun to bring the gum wrappers to church and fold them inside her bag, much to her mother's chagrin. It was a kind of meditation, and she believed in it more than in any of the prayers of the rosary. Delia would never think of church as a sacred, holy place again.

Her mother's hawk-like eyes scanned the congregation for any sign that Delia's cracks might be showing.

Attention for attention's sake was never her mother's intent.

Delia had decided it wasn't worth it to argue about going to confession year after year, and by the time she was sixteen, she barely spoke, just came downstairs wearing her thickest snow pants and, underneath them, layers of leggings.

Now it was June, and nobody seemed to notice anything odd, but by this point Delia had perfected being apart from everyone, even herself. Her eyes were glazed, and if she managed it just right – *whoop* – she was out of her body, looking down from a place where nobody could touch her.

Even her brother just stared out the window of the car as they drove to Mass, while she watched herself sitting next to him, folding wrappers, fitting the Vs together, sweating profusely in her Gore-Tex snow pants.

He was too full of himself now that he was a rodeo

star. The only things he noticed were his reputation and his fancy Appaloosa–Quarter Horse mix, Maverick. Their father had bought Maverick with cash, as if he were just another pair of boots.

At the rodeos, girls lined up for miles to take their picture with Maverick and her brother, but mostly with her brother. Delia knew he was almost too handsome for his own good. He had begun to swagger and walk the way Hank did, as if there were a horse under him at all times.

He could not seem to lose any rodeo event he entered, and had even appeared in a magazine, *Western Horseman*, which had restored that proud glint in her mother's eye for at least a month afterward.

Who wouldn't be a rodeo star if they spent every waking hour down at the corral, running patterns, jumping barrels? Delia's brother was meticulous in his training, and not a penny was spared to ensure that he would be the best. The boy who had once tried to find the most colourful gum wrappers for her and who'd done anything to keep her from crying was now sitting next to her in the car, yet Delia couldn't get him to notice that she was dressed for a blizzard.

It didn't matter. The real Delia was floating above them, too far away to care. She was a tiny speck next to the sun as it beat down from the dazzling Wyoming sky. She was higher than the Wind River Range, or the Bighorn Mountains, or even the Grand Tetons. Delia, the other Delia, the one inside the car whose brother refused to notice anymore, just laughed and laughed and laughed, heating up the windows as if they were sitting in a pressure cooker.

And then one day, Father Monster just up and left. A new priest arrived from India with a thick accent that barely anyone could understand, and nobody mentioned Father Lazaria again except to say he'd been 'reassigned'.

Delia's first thought was that God had not abandoned her after all. But that was instantly replaced with another thought that was not so easy to shake: *Why did He take so long?*

Her old babysitter, Michelle, came to visit out of the blue, with an engagement ring on her finger, saying she'd thought about Delia a lot over the years. Delia was sceptical. She could think of nothing to talk about, so she showed Michelle the gum chain, which when rolled up was the size of a volleyball.

Michelle couldn't believe it. 'I just got busy with the rest of my life and totally forgot even how to do this. But you might have a world record here.'

Delia remembered the way Michelle had gotten busy with 'being a teenager and everything'. Now it was the rest of her life.

'I guess you forgot about me, too,' Delia said. Her eyes had no light behind them.

'What happened?' asked Michelle quietly.

Delia just shook her head.

'Whatever it is, it's not your fault,' said Michelle.

'People always say that,' said Delia, 'but they don't mean it.'

'Where's the spunky girl I babysat all those years ago?' asked Michelle gently.

Delia realised she sounded rude. Michelle obviously sensed that Delia wasn't that happy to see her.

'You were my favourite babysitter,' she said, but it was a feeble attempt.

'I'm sorry I stayed away so long. The little girl I knew would have fought her way out of anything. I do know that. She's still in there, isn't she?'

Michelle leaned forward and lightly tapped Delia's shirt, just over her heart. Her engagement ring sparkled. Delia tried not to flinch.

A few months later she'd walked into her brother's room to ask if she could ride Maverick. Not far, just around the corral.

Her brother was sobbing facedown into his pillow, and she recognised it for what it was. She knew that kind of crying, that curling into a foetal position. The way a person's body holds grief and fear, and the shaking that comes from keeping it all inside until it's just too much. It finally spills out and cannot be contained, even by the most expensive cotton pillowcases in the house.

She lay down beside him, matching the question-mark shape of his body with her own in silent acknowledgement. In recognition.

'He has a list,' her brother said after what seemed like hours of just lying next to each other. 'It's inside his Bible. A long, long list, as if he's so proud of himself.'

His voice was like ice cracking on a frozen pond.

'Your name is in there. But I believed you from the first, Delia. I really did. I just knew it was pointless to say anything. And then it was me, and what would people say, how could that happen to a boy who was ranked first in the state in pole bending and barrel racing? I just hoped maybe he wasn't hurting you anymore. And then you came down in your snow pants, and I knew.'

So he had noticed.

She tightened her arm around his chest, breathing into his wide back that smelled of hay and horses. Her beautiful, broken rodeo star of a brother. He had found his own way of coping, and she had to admit, it looked a lot saner than clinging to a gum chain.

He'd also fooled her. He'd fooled everyone.

But even the best contortionists can fit into those tiny boxes for only so long.

His record had recently been shattered by a total unknown from Kansas whose horse had the most impressive hind end Delia had ever seen.

Her brother and Maverick had been expected to win easily, but they hadn't even placed at this year's National High School Finals Rodeo.

She thought he'd just run the patterns too often and Maverick had grown bored by the time the event rolled around. But now she knew the real reason: her brother's mind had worked and reworked a pattern of its own; nothing to do with a rodeo.

Delia knew that pattern.

She knew how it made you question everything else about yourself, even things you were good at. It could destroy you.

He was right that it was pointless to talk because nobody listens to boys who seem untouchable or little girls who speak up.

But the thing about little girls is that one day they aren't little anymore.

So Delia began to plan.

She disguised her voice and made phone calls to men who were higher and higher up in the church. She praised her missing priest for guiding her on the right path, she wanted to send him a card of thanks, how might she find his address?

It was almost too easy.

Her praise was like oil, greasing the wheels of information on the other end of the phone line. 'Oh, he's been many places,' she was finally told one day. 'Let's see: Alaska, Minnesota, Wyoming . . . but we've moved him again. One moment, dear.'

Delia didn't understand why she was the one who had to act. Why hadn't anyone protected them or stood up for them or at the very least believed her when she spoke out years ago? Waiting for help had been her first mistake. But Michelle was right about one thing: Delia was a fighter. She wasn't waiting anymore.

She heard a file cabinet being opened, papers rustling.

'Most recently Granville, a tiny mining town in Colorado. He'll be so happy to get your card, Miss – what did you say your name was?'

Click.

Delia scribbled 'Granville' on the inside of a matchbook.

She slept all night on the bus with her hood up and a switchblade in her boot, between her sock and shin. Inside her backpack, her gum chain was now forty feet long. It was a stupid, simple thing, but it was a part of her, like a beating heart she carried outside her body. She wanted to keep it close. For now.

Her plan went as far as getting herself to the door of the Granville Catholic church, but after that she didn't have a clue. It was time to act, and still she was unsure – until she saw the schedule tacked to the door.

Father Lazaria was hearing confessions from noon to one.

Oh, the irony!

She slid into the pew closest to the door and looked up at the stone walls, the stained-glass windows with the midday light cutting across the etched faces of disciples and followers of Christ. She wondered whose daddy had paid for these windows and what else had they cost? The church had meant so much to her, until it hadn't.

Was there a little girl here in Granville who was feeling like the chosen one? Did that little girl have a brother? Or a mother who cared more about what people thought than about keeping her children safe?

Delia knew that on one side of the confessional was the priest, waiting to hear the sins of his sheep.

The wolves have been in charge long enough, she thought, slipping into the box. She was supposed to say, 'Forgive me, Father, for I have sinned . . .'

She didn't say anything. She waited.

'My child,' said the voice that had haunted her, that had driven a wedge between her and her parents; that had broken her brother. The voice she wished she could forget, now a long fingernail running down the chalkboard of her spine.

'How long has it been since your last confession?'

'How long has it been since yours?' she said, pushing her hand through the hole that had been placed right above the kneeler, just like she knew it would be. But this time she was armed. She flipped the blade open with an ominous click and pressed it hard against his crotch. She hoped it was the last time she would ever get this close to him.

'Don't move,' she warned. 'Or you will regret it.'

She thought about the little girl Michelle had known, the one who would fight back against anything.

'This is what being helpless feels like,' she said.

He wheezed, disgusting nose hairs whistling with fear. He did not want her to hurt him, and she realised now, that wasn't why she'd come. She just wanted to make him afraid of what she *might* do.

'If you ever threaten another child or even think about threatening another child, I will hunt you down. I will find you. Give me your robe.'

Yes, that little girl was still in there, even if her voice was rusty and shaky from lack of use.

She heard him struggling to disrobe in the tiny confessional while also trying to avoid the switchblade. She pulled the fabric through the hole, feeling like a magician tugging on an ever-growing silk scarf.

She knew he would be transferred again, that the church would always cover for him. But he deserved to be afraid.

'Don't hurt me. Please,' he begged.

She had done what she came to do.

She told him to stay in the confessional for at least an hour after she was gone. Somehow she knew he would stay much longer than that.

She set the robe on fire behind the Piggly Wiggly on the edge of town and threw it into the dumpster. It was white, not the purple one he'd worn all those years ago. She remembered how he'd raised his purple arms and it had made her think of a phoenix, the mythological bird that burns to ash and then rises from the flames. She hoped nothing evil would be reincarnated from these ashes.

She wouldn't need her gum chain anymore. She threw it on top of the smoking robe, thinking of how many painful hours she had spent making it, days upon days, years upon years. Ashes to ashes, dust to dust.

From a pay phone she made one more call to the archbishop's office, the same one that had naively given her Father Monster's address. She told the nasal voice to stay on the line, because she wanted him to hear the names of Father Lazaria's victims, one by one, from his own Bible. It was a horrifically long list.

Minnie, Jasmine, Mary, Michael . . .

She heard the breathing on the other end of the phone grow distant and said if he stopped listening before she was finished, she would call the police.

And if the church let Father Lazaria near children again, she would do so much worse than that.

She read each name slowly and clearly, trying to give every person the dignity they deserved. She didn't know all the names, but she recognised some of them, remembering what her mother had said about these things not happening in their world.

She stumbled only once, not on her own name, but on her brother's: Silas.

Afterward she walked for about a mile away from town before sticking out her thumb, barely noticing the faint scent of smoke in the air.

Basketball Town

The world is on fire. The summer of 1995 will go on record as the first summer in history that folks in Lared, Montana, finally have something besides basketball to talk about. The skies are clogged with smoke billowing in from Colorado and Wyoming, an apocalypse of ash and soot. It's so dark, streetlights come on in the middle of the day. Weather advisories warn against exercising outside because of the inordinate amount of harmful particulates in the air. Nobody has taken a real breath in days, and everybody is cranky.

For Kelsey Randolph, not being able to play basketball ten hours a day on the outdoor court is basically the end of the world.

She pushes through the doors of the U-Pump-It, bracing for her usual reception from Jimmy Jeffs. But for the first time, JJ doesn't notice her. Nobody notices her. A small group is clustered beneath a television set mounted over the candy aisle, watching the news.

'Goddamn lunatic,' JJ says, not taking his eyes off the screen.

Two men in funny tall hats are leading a confused-looking priest out of a rectory and into a waiting black car. The volume is too low to hear the reporter, but words scroll beneath the image: 'Colorado Priest Accused of Accidentally Starting Blaze That Has Grown to Over Seven Thousand Acres'.

'Burned his robes up in a dumpster and started the wildfire,' Jimmy says. 'Crazy as a loon.'

Kelsey feels an unexpected wave of sympathy for the priest, who looks shaken and disoriented. She doesn't know anything about Catholics but figures the bigger the hat, the higher the rank. Those men on either side of him must be in charge.

Kelsey's stranger gauge isn't well honed. Having grown up in Lared, population 750, she finds that her default is usually to trust people, even if there is the odd Jimmy Jeffs to contend with.

'If that was anyone else, they'd be going to jail,' JJ says in the authoritative voice of someone who has been faced many times with the prospect of going to jail. 'Now they'll just take him to some comfy retirement home to live out his days.'

'He doesn't look dangerous, just old,' Kelsey says, without thinking.

JJ turns to look at her.

'What do you know about dangerous? And how's him setting fire to the world gonna help your jump shot?'

'I'm at pump three.' She waves a ten-dollar bill in his face.

'You know, if you'd just taken that shot from the top of the key, we would have won.'

She grabs a Snickers bar off the rack and stuffs it into her pocket as soon as he turns his back. (Everybody does it: payment for having to deal with JJ.) He's oblivious to everything once he's up on his soapbox, ranting about Kelsey's jump shot or accusing her of not shooting enough. Or insisting that because of her, they'd lost a game last year for the first time since anyone can remember. One game. You'd think she'd killed someone and hidden the body, the way everyone was acting.

'I know you think it's your job to feed your forwards, but guards also need to know when to *take the shot*.' He emphasises every word with a finger punch to the register.

'Assists are nice, but nobody wins a game because they got *one more assist* than the other guy.'

After a long pause and a longer lingering glance at her boobs, he adds, 'Or gal.'

He takes her money and waggles his tongue back and forth through the space where his front teeth should be.

Why, oh why, isn't there another gas station in this town?

'Thanks, JJ.' She waves at him, using the Snickers bar as her middle finger. The bell ding-dongs overhead, and she pushes through the broken doors, crisscrossed with masking tape and cardboard, because why fix them? Jimmy Jeff's customers will just break them again; they're dependable like that.

'Shoot the damn ball!' he shouts.

Inside her car, Kelsey turns on the wipers and watches a thin layer of ash swish across her windshield like grey snow. This summer is a disaster, and not just because of the fire.

She really misses her cousin Lillian, who has only sent two postcards and has not apologised for leaving without saying goodbye.

Lil loves Alaska, says it's just like Montana but bigger in every way: bigger mountains, bigger skies, bigger belt buckles, as if that's possible. She doesn't know that fires have choked all the life out of the wide Montana sky; she's too busy writing poetry and plucking freezing-cold children out of a glacier-fed lake.

She hadn't even asked Kelsey to go with her when she applied to be a counsellor at Camp Wildwood, but of course they both knew it was impossible. No way could Kelsey miss two months of basketball. Still, Lillian could have asked. It was their inside joke, that even weirdos like to be invited. Although normally the joke referred to Lillian, who had not inherited the basketball gene like almost everyone else in Lared.

Lillian was not part of the inner circle that revolved around practices and away games and huge parades every year, that celebrated the Lared Lynx and their many, many state titles. Parades on Main Street were so prevalent, they were boring (according to Lillian), punctuated by balloons and marching bands and the players riding in Cal Worthington's pink Cadillac, waving their state trophy – year after year – while a sea of maroon-and-gold supporters lined the streets.

That's what it meant to be born into a town drunk on basketball. Everyone, in some way, was blessed, touched, or, at the very least, obsessed with basketball.

Everyone except Lillian.

There must have been others like Lillian over the years, but if there had been, Kelsey didn't know them. The ones who couldn't catch on, no matter how many 'little dribbler' camps their parents signed them up for. If someone didn't have talent, they usually found other ways to ride the maroon-and-gold wave, usually as scorekeepers, managers, cheerleaders, or band members, or even just by being really, really loud in the stands.

It might not seem possible that everyone in one town was a basketball fanatic, but it was the God's-honest truth in Lared.

So much so that Lillian had to transfer to the high school in the next town over just to get away. But she'd been born into a basketball family, and unless she emancipated herself and moved to another country – or Alaska – there was nowhere to hide.

Kelsey loved her cousin to pieces, but she also feared for her. And secretly – until recently, anyway – had thanked her lucky stars that she was one of the blessed, because she didn't want to live her life like Lillian, a seal floating out to sea on a rapidly melting iceberg.

Although when she had said that to Lillian, her cousin had spurted soda out of her nose and howled with laughter.

'Careful, Kels. Your very own metaphor is going to sneak up and bite you in the butt.'

Kelsey had been confused by the laughter and thought perhaps Lil just hadn't understood what she'd meant. Since they lived in landlocked Montana, anything involving the ocean was a bit of a stretch. But metaphors were more Lillian's terrain, to be fair.

They were at the Frosty Freez, the halfway point between their two schools, looking forward to the free food that was owed to someone of Kelsey's stature. So many unspoken rules, it would be a difficult place to understand if you hadn't been born here. Or in Lillian's case, even if you had been, but at least she understood what she didn't know, if that made any sense.

'Hot fudge sundae for my cousin?' Lillian said, smiling sweetly at the skinny waiter who gave Kelsey's maroon-and-gold warm-up jacket a cold look. He was from the rival school, the same one Lillian had transferred into. They had never won a state title, although they'd come closer than any other team in the past four years. But the Plateau High Buffaloes still weren't the Lared Lynx, because nobody was. Even a mere waiter at Frosty Freez who had no stake whatsoever in the game would know what was what. He squirmed visibly but tried to sound like he couldn't be bothered.

'Like I care about the Lynx point guard?' he muttered, setting two sodas on the table.

Lillian's elbow knocked over the soda nearest to her. Nobody could say it wasn't an accident.

'Oh, I'm so, so sorry,' she said as Kelsey tried not to laugh. Soda dripped onto the floor and seeped into the brown shag.

'I'll bring you another one,' he said, in a tone that implied he absolutely would not be bringing another one, as he wiped his arm on his apron and kicked ice cubes into a corner to melt under a potted plastic plant.

'Don't forget the sundae,' Lil called after him, 'or we could just get a manager . . .'

Behind his back he flipped her the bird.

'There's a gentleman for you,' Kelsey said, pouring

half of her soda into Lil's glass, since he obviously wouldn't be coming back.

'My one little bit of athleticism at work there,' said Lil, wiping her sticky jeans with a napkin and giving Kelsey an impish grin.

'Whatever would I do without you?' said Kelsey.

'I guess you'll find out soon enough.'

And that was when Lil had told her: Alaska. Summer camp. Three months away, where she wouldn't have to hear one goddamn word about basketball. At least, she hoped not.

'But you still fit in here, Lil,' Kelsey had said. 'Look at you with the soda.'

It was almost the truth, but it sounded weak once she'd said it. Worse, it sounded patronising.

'Kelsey, don't you ever wonder what's going to happen to you when you're no longer a Lynx?'

'College.' Kelsey shrugged, her mouth full of curly fries.

'Yeah, but only to play ball. You don't even know what you'll major in.'

'Doesn't matter. I already got a scholarship to Montana State.'

'And then after college? You're going to move back here and have ten kids with your Lynx boyfriend? Who, I might add, is only your boyfriend because you're both point guards, which is the least romantic thing ever.'

'Hey, hitting kind of close to home, aren't you?'

'Yes, my point exactly,' said Lillian. 'We need to kill this ridiculous dysfunctional genetic *disease*.'

Their fathers were brothers who had married their high school sweethearts, who were also alums of the Lady Lynx. (The girls' team was just called Lynx now, same as the guys'. Feminism and all that.)

Kelsey laughed. 'It's an obsession, but I think calling it a disease is a bit of a stretch.'

'If you could only see yourself,' Lillian said. 'I'm not the weird one here, Kelsey, not by a long shot.'

'I never said you were.'

'How's that sea ice treating you? I hope you can swim as well as you play ball, Kels.'

'Lillian, come on . . .'

But she was gone. Just like that. She'd thrown her book bag over her shoulder and walked out of the Frosty Freez, leaving Kelsey feeling slapped by her own metaphor and also bailing on the bill.

Lillian had left for Alaska a few days afterward, and now she was writing postcards about mountains and lakes and clean air. All things that existed in Montana, too, if wildfire smoke wasn't obscuring the view.

Or if you lived anywhere other than Lared, where the latest plan was to wear green surgical masks to play ball outside.

When Kelsey pulled up to the courts a few minutes

late (thanks, JJ), she couldn't help noticing that her teammates looked like escapees from the nearest hospital. They were lined up shooting free throws. Every time someone bounced the ball, puffs of ash flew into the air like dust bombs. Babs, the Lynx all-star forward, had also donned a pair of ski goggles. Kelsey couldn't tell if anyone was laughing, because their mouths were obscured by the green masks, but she knew one person who would think this was hilarious.

Glancing at the passenger seat, she almost expected to see Lillian, notebook and pen in hand, eyes rolling to prove her point. 'This town is so myopic, if the world was ending, the only worry would be how to get in ten more minutes of court time.'

On the seat there was just the Snickers wrapper and the postcards from a distant land – as if her cousin's ghost had decided to haunt her through the postal service. Lil wrote about the wildflowers, fireweed and columbine and skunk cabbage. She said foxglove was her favourite but it was poisonous, and believe it or not, you had to watch the younger campers, who were known to eat things they shouldn't.

I wish you were here, Kels, but I realise it's hard to imagine you doing anything else, anywhere else. I guess I'll just have to see the world for the both of us. Love, Lil.

Where does Kelsey see herself in a year, two, five? She sees nothing but smoky, swirling ash.

There's a tap on the window. Her father's eyes are quizzical over his green mask, his brow furrowed. Is she going to play?

She has those same eyes; can widen them the way he does to answer, can mirror him in so many ways.

Yes, of course she's going to play. What else would she do? She tries not to hold his gaze too long, afraid there will be something in it that will make her question herself. She cares what he thinks and has felt uncertain about how he sees her since the season ended. Since that one loss.

Her father is one of the best referees in the state. His brother, Lillian's dad, is one of the best coaches. Right out of college, they stepped into their roles as easily as they'd stepped into their high-top sneakers all their lives – the laces untied, never taking them off, sometimes even sleeping with them on.

When Kelsey and her brothers were little, their mom had loaded up the station wagon with bags of Cheetos and coolers full of Wonder Bread sandwiches and soda and they'd driven all over Montana to watch her dad ref. So many hazy memories, surrounded by sweaty brothers all stretched out in sleeping bags in the back of the car, waking up in time for the next game. Montana dust coating the back window, grazing their skin, their clothes, as if an invisible hand were tossing fistfuls of sand at them as they drove across the state. The sun blistering orange in the heat of the day.

Everything in her memory was tinged with orange, their Cheeto-y fingers and Orange Crush tongues. They were the dishevelled kids with constant bed head, yelling from the bleachers in Billings, Helena, Bozeman, and places so tiny they were left off the maps. Small-town gymnasiums with hard wooden bleachers and oversized mascots, like chickens with big feet and tissue-paper feathers, that sometimes made them laugh, while others sometimes caused their mother to tut and shake her head, or worse, leave the gym.

Once, Kelsey's mother had made her and her brothers wait in the car because one of the teams called themselves the Redskins and had an Indian mascot with long braids and a feathered headdress who ran up and down the sidelines wielding a tomahawk.

'I will not let you just sit and watch this hideous display of racism,' she told them. 'It is demeaning and wrong and don't you ever forget it.'

'But it's cold out here,' her brother had whined.

'Good. I hope you're uncomfortable, because that's nothing compared to how kids from Rocky Boy or Crow or Flathead must feel when they play here,' their mother said. 'Put on your damn coat if you're cold.'

Kelsey would not forget it, nor would she forget the

screaming parents who sometimes jumped right out of the bleachers to get into her father's face, his whistle blaring, sweat darkening his back and the armpits of his zebra-striped jersey. She loved that he was the one who could make people cheer happily or scream with anger – he and his whistle spurred more emotion than any preacher she had ever seen yelling from a pulpit. It was thrilling to behold.

But that was when she was a little kid and her only role in any of it had been to eat popcorn and stomp her feet on the bleachers when the cheerleaders asked the crowd to join in, trying to distract an opposing free throw or psych up the defence. It was loud and stinky and exciting. But mostly, Kelsey had been cheering for the ref, the guy in the stripes, the one with the whistle and the eyes that matched her own. She could not imagine a more perfect world than the one she'd grown up in.

Until high school, when she learned quickly that nobody cheers for the ref. Least of all his daughter, who would prefer that he not notice every move she made.

'You just have to be better than everyone else,' he said when she complained. 'Because the fans are watching me harder when I'm reffing my own daughter's game.'

'But that travelling call was bananas! Those girls were double-teaming me and hacking like crazy. Intentional fouling!'

'I don't care if they were acting like boxers in a ring. If you don't want me to call travelling, then you better cement your pivot foot. Even if they draw blood, if you move that foot, I'm calling it a walk. The burden of proof is on you when I'm the ref.'

Lillian had been sitting in Kelsey's kitchen, listening. Lillian had also been there when the whole thing happened, sitting in the bleachers, watching her cousin get called for travelling by her own father. There was a word for all this, Kelsey thought. Nepotism? No, that meant you were somehow benefiting from being related – and this was the opposite.

Kelsey was embarrassed that Lillian had heard the details of the call play out in her dining room. Lillian and her father never had to have these kinds of fights. Their relationship had never been so idealistic; there was no 'falling from grace' for Lillian.

It was the first time an idea began to worm its way into Kelsey's head: Had her cousin's lack of basketball skills actually been a small gift, rather than a curse?

This idea was jarring, but still, it began to take root in Kelsey's brain as Lillian got farther and farther away, becoming someone who could choose any path, someone for whom there were no expectations.

Kelsey, on the other hand, was feeling Lared close in around her.

She had never felt so much pressure to be perfect, until she began to make mistakes.

Kelsey had always blamed the messenger. But Lillian was not here to shine her strange illuminating light, revealing things that Kelsey refused to see.

Now there was no one between her and the message. She felt abandoned. Lost.

Her father tapped again on her window, and for the first time in her life, Kelsey decided that she didn't feel like hitting the court. It wasn't worth it to put on a stupid surgical mask and squint through the gritty air trying to find the basket or someone to pass to.

She shook her head, started up her car, and waved goodbye to the one person she had never said no to.

She drove around town for half an hour, which meant she'd basically gone in circles, passing the same houses about a hundred times until she wound up at her boyfriend's place, which she never did in the middle of the day. Usually they were both busy playing ball.

'Hi,' said Brian, surprised to see Kelsey in his doorway. 'Come on in. Want some milk?'

He was drinking straight out of a gallon jug. His jersey was completely soaked, front and back. One high-top was on, unlaced; the other foot was half in, half out of a sweat sock.

'Where did you play?' she asked.

'Our coach opened the gym,' he said. 'You know, because of the bad air.'

'We're playing outside,' she said.

'Yeah, well, we're the guys,' he laughed, as if that was funny. Or made any sense.

She was still standing in the doorway.

'Kels, you're letting in the dregs. In or out, I need to shut the door.'

She stepped inside as a coughing attack hit her.

It happened to everyone lately: coughing as if they smoked a pack a day. It was the new normal.

Brian rubbed her back between her shoulder blades as she leaned forward and hacked her lungs out.

'Thanks,' she said, standing up, wiping her eyes.

He didn't have a particularly pretty face, and his nose was off a bit to the left from the time he'd been elbowed getting a rebound in junior high – four years ago – but he and Kelsey had been a couple ever since. She had fallen hard for him, watching him fall hard to the floor, his broken nose spurting blood everywhere. He hadn't let go of the ball, even while bleeding all over his white jersey. Blood was on the gym floor and on the guy that elbowed him. Her heart had beaten wildly in her chest – as if something were blooming inside her – watching him make both of his free throws. Lillian had laughed at her then for falling in love over a rebound.

'It was so much more than a rebound,' Kelsey had said at the time.

But today Brian just looked sweaty. And smelled bad.

'I still don't understand why we play outside and you get the gym.'

'Calm down,' he said. 'We're going to trade off. Your dad put up a real stink about it.'

'You mean my uncle,' she said. 'Our coach.'

'No, I mean your dad. I heard him getting heated when we were warming up.'

'Well, he knows he's not supposed to interfere. It's against the rules for a ref to be involved in team practices.'

'I guess he cares more about his precious daughter's lungs than he does about the rules.'

Again, Brian seemed to think he was being funny. Was he always like this? Suddenly Kelsey wasn't sure.

'Are you being snide on purpose?' she asked.

'Are you having your period?'

'Fuck you.'

'What's gotten into you?' He backed away, arms in the air, as if she were on the attack.

'I just want to talk and you're jumping on me with these one-liners that aren't funny, Brian.'

'Well, usually you think they are. Now you're acting more like ...'

'More like what?'

'More like ... Lillian. The way she never laughs at anything.'

Kelsey said nothing. Her throat was scratchy, like she'd been standing too close to a campfire. She kept trying to clear it, aware that she sounded like a cat hacking up a fur ball.

'Maybe I'll go,' she said, once she found her voice.

'Yeah, good idea,' he said, not bothering to pretend he cared, shutting the door behind her.

Back in her car, she thought about what he'd said. Lillian never laughed at anything?

It wasn't true. Lillian was the only person who could make Kelsey laugh so hard she peed her pants. For as long as she could remember, before they knew that Kelsey would be the basketball star and Lillian would be the oddball, they'd just been cousins who saw themselves as the yin to the other's yang.

Their fathers had started them early, when the basketballs were almost as big as they were, and they would laugh and tumble over them in saggy diapers, like rolling around with a light pumpkin, getting it stuck between their pudgy legs.

Kelsey can still hear Lillian's deep belly laugh and remember how contagious it was, how once they got going they could not stop. She imagines, but doesn't remember, that their fathers would roll their eyes and shake their heads. Probably in fear that one of their children would not shake off the silliness and transition into the real thing, dribbling, doing figure eights, butterfly drills.

Those drills slowly began to make sense to Kelsey but not to Lillian. It was like watching a generational rope unravel, so gradually that it would have gone unnoticed except that each person in the Randolph family had easily wrapped themselves around the strand before them, creating an unbreakable bond. It was hard to believe that one person could unravel it.

Kelsey's talent compared to Lillian's clumsiness led to a rift between their fathers. Neither one knew what to say, so they didn't talk about it.

But this was Basketball Town; it wasn't a subject you could just pretend wasn't there.

It was always Lillian who refused to believe that they had to keep playing this charade, that basketball was the only thing that mattered. She was the equivalent of the little kid who keeps yelling, 'The emperor has no clothes,' except in Lared there was usually a marching band drowning her out.

Kelsey heard Lillian's voice all the time now. Watching her teammates wearing green surgical masks, hearing Brian say the boys deserved the gym and she was just 'having her period' if she disagreed, the way her father was overstepping his bounds as ref. Kelsey was full of questions that Lillian wasn't even there to pose. So they must have been coming from inside her own mind.

She opened the glove box and pulled out the second postcard from her cousin. It was a long skinny one. A picture of a mountain ringed with fog took up the whole front. 'The highest peak in North America'.

You should have been here, Kels. I woke up and kids were missing from their beds, which is pretty much a counsellor's worst nightmare. But it's light out all night, so at least searching for them was easy. I couldn't believe where they were. The stupid outside court with the dirt floor, huge potholes in it and an old pickle barrel for a basket. I have never seen basketball played like this. First of all, they were terrible – even worse than me! Just laughing and falling in the dirt and trying to put the ball through that stupid smelly bucket. But it was also absolute joy. I didn't think it was possible to play basketball that way, not for glory or attention but just for the thing itself. These kids surprise me every day. Love, Lil

Kelsey drove with Lillian's words swirling around and around her head: 'just for the thing itself.'

At home, her mother was waiting in the entryway. Her scrunched face made Kelsey wonder instantly what she had done. Her mother rarely got mad, but her moral compass was finely tuned, and her eyebrows were pointing due north, a sign that Kelsey had done something drastic. But she couldn't think what.

'Jimmy Jeffs called.'

'Mom, everyone—'

'Do not "everyone does it" me, young lady. You know better. Get in my car. We are going back to pay for a Snickers bar.'

'It was literally like fifty-seven cents.'

'Really, Kelsey? Who do you think you are? And for that matter, who do you think I am? This is about self-respect, not fifty-goddamn-seven cents.'

Her mother had a habit of swearing when she was taking some kind of parental high ground. It was confusingly contradictory.

'Fine, I'll pay for the stupid candy bar.'

'Oh, you buckle up, young lady. This is going to cost you a lot more than fifty-seven cents.'

Kelsey stared at her mother's profile as she drove. She had one dimple, and when she was mad it pulsed in her cheek, as if that was where she kept her heart. She'd been a fabulous basketball player in her day, but now she was thick in the middle and limped a little from arthritis in her left hip.

'Too many hip checks against those Wyoming girls, the ones that grew up on ranches,' she'd always say.

'God knows they must have practised against black Angus cattle.'

Whenever Kelsey played against a Wyoming team her mother would offer the same advice: 'Just set your feet. Don't lean or move your hips.' As if Kelsey didn't know how to take an offensive foul.

Her mother might be angry at the moment, but Lillian's postcard was fresh in Kelsey's mind, and she couldn't stop herself from asking questions.

'Mom, do you miss playing ball?'

She looked like she was thinking hard about whether to answer.

'Yeah. Yeah, I do.'

'What do you miss most?'

'Are you trying to distract me? You are not getting out of this, Kelsey.'

'As if, Mom. I'm not that dumb. I honestly want to know.'

'Hmmmm. Well, I loved that feeling you get, you know the one? When the whole team is like a well-oiled machine and you execute a play like clockwork. I can still feel that sometimes, watching you girls. Watching each person like a cog in a machine, doing what it takes for the whole thing to come together. It's like magic. I love that.'

'But if you were all alone, just playing, say, by yourself, and nobody watched, would you love it?'

Her mother glanced at her as if this was a trick question.

'Want to know a secret? That I've never told anyone?'

Kelsey shrugged. Yes, she desperately wanted to know a secret.

'I loved it so much. I used to sleep with my arm around the basketball, just so I could breathe in that dirty orange-leather smell.'

'That's your secret?' Kelsey was a little disappointed.

'No, that's not it.'

She pulled the car to the side of the road and put it in park. Then she turned to face Kelsey, wincing a little as her hip twisted underneath her.

'This is my secret: Sometimes I feel so guilty that we loved it so much, we didn't want it to end. And we keep living out that thing we can't let go of through our children, trying to make it last. But I wonder sometimes if it's fair, this thing we do.'

'Really?'

'I've watched you your whole life. Your talent is beyond believable, and I tell myself, *She's got such a gift*. But sometimes I look at your face while you're out there, and I wonder.'

'What do you mean?'

'Just wonder who you're doing it for. See you looking around a lot. And I think, *My baby is too concerned about what other people think.* I don't see you feeling it the way I felt it. Like it's magic.'

'It just doesn't feel like magic when I'm so worried about letting my own father down. It's like his job is at stake if I make a mistake. What's the fun in that?'

'Honey, I do hear you. That makes perfect sense, so—'

She was going to say something else, but Kelsey cut her off.

'Can you be good at something and maybe not love it?'

'Is this about something Lillian said?'

'No. I mean, I thought so once. But this is about me. I've been wondering more about doing what I love and not just going along with what everyone expects. But it's hard to separate the two.'

Wind was blowing dust and tumbleweeds across the road. It had become almost normal, to live amid swirly grey ash, smelling smoke. Normal is whatever you grow used to, like wildfires choking the life out of everything. Or a town that lives through its children, over and over again, until nobody remembers a time when that wasn't the case.

'Your dad's been trying to talk to you all day.'

'I know. I know I'm in trouble for skipping out on practice.'

'No. No, you're not.'

144

'What, then?'

'Well, he wanted to tell you himself, but I'll just nip this one in the bud. He's not going to ref this season.'

'Why not?'

Not ref? That was like saying her father would no longer need his organs.

'Why would he do that?'

'So you can have a senior year like a normal person. It's too much pressure, having your dad be the one that makes the calls. And you just said so yourself, so obviously he's not stupid.'

'So he's giving up what he loves for me?'

'I think you are what he loves, Kelsey.'

Kelsey leaned into her then, breathing into her mom's neck, which actually did smell a bit like old basketball leather.

Just when she thought she might start crying, her mom said, 'Now, enough of this nonsense. Come on, you're going to be late for your first shift.'

Kelsey had hoped she might have forgotten all about the U-Pump-It and Jimmy Jeffs, but of course, that would have made her someone else's mother.

'Excuse me, what shift?'

'You heard me. I told JJ you'd be working for him the rest of the summer, which by my count is about fifty-seven more days, so a penny a day and you'll have paid off that debt.'

'Have you lost your mind?'

'Honey, after those Wyoming girls got done with me, that's about all I have left,' she said, laughing and steering the car back onto the road. A tumbleweed stuck to the undercarriage made a scratching sound along the pavement, like background music in a horror movie, which Kelsey felt was appropriate.

'We will love you until the end of time no matter what you do,' she said, 'but my children will not steal. And don't you forget it.'

Kelsey thought back to her brother complaining about the game they were made to sit out in the cold car, because of the racist mascot. She did not want to have to see Jimmy Jeffs every day, but you had to hand it to her mother when she said, 'There are some things more important than you being comfortable.' She meant it.

Alaska Was Wasted on Us

'Your camper pooped his pants and threw them in a tree,' Amy says to Fiona.

'Oh God, was it Nick?'

'Yeah. His brother, Franky, said he was going to try to hold it all week, but he couldn't. I think he's pretty terrified of the outhouses. Especially the one named Forget-Me-Not.'

Fiona is sure Nick is terrified of all the outhouses – Lupin, Fireweed, Foxglove. Whoever had come up with the brilliant idea to name them after wildflowers didn't have a clue about six-year-olds.

'Can you help me get them down?' asks Fiona, staring into the branches.

'I have nineteen other campers to worry about right now,' says Amy in an agitated tone.

'Right,' says Fiona. 'I've got it.'

Amy is obviously still mad at her about losing their jobs at Dairy Queen. But she'll come around; she always does. Fiona just needs to be patient. She wishes Amy were more grateful, though, that Fiona found them both positions here at Camp Wildwood for the summer, even if they are totally unqualified.

Camp counsellors needed, Alaskans preferred. Outdoor experience a plus but not necessary.

'Look, we tick all the boxes!' she'd said, showing Amy the ad.

'Especially the "no outdoor experience necessary" box,' said Amy sarcastically. 'Have you forgotten that the outdoors is full of mosquitoes, Fiona? And also, I hate children.'

'No, you don't,' said Fiona. 'You were one yourself once.'

She couldn't understand why Amy cared so much about Dairy Queen anyway. Greasy fast food with perverts for coworkers? She should really be thanking Fiona.

Although, now that she's standing under the branches of a spruce tree dying from beetle kill and staring up at Nick's jeans, Fiona is almost nostalgic for her plaid uniform with the little bobble on the cap. And she loves Peanut Buster Parfaits more than she loves other people's kids, though she definitely doesn't hate kids. And neither does Amy, she thinks as she finally manages to retrieve the soiled green jeans with a long broom handle. She takes them to the staff cabin to wrap in a plastic garbage bag. They'll need to go in a bear-proof container until the end of camp. If they haven't disintegrated by then.

Lillian, a counsellor from Montana, is sitting alone at a table writing postcards. She glances up, gives Fiona half a wave, and keeps writing.

Fiona smiles. Lillian is such a relief. She has no secret agenda like several of the other counsellors from the Lower 48, who are either environmental activists or animal-rights activists or some other kind of activist that Fiona and Amy hadn't even known existed. Like the girl who said pulling carrots out of the ground was cruel.

Fiona had thought she was joking and had laughed hysterically until Amy jabbed her in the ribs with her finger.

'You didn't have to poke me so hard,' said Fiona.

'Well, you were giving her the stand-up comic of the year award with that laugh. You needed more than a nudge.'

Anyway, thank goodness for Lillian. She's easygoing, funny, helpful – as long as nobody asks her to bring her campers to the basketball courts.

Fiona had asked her what she had against basketball and Lillian had just rolled her eyes and said, 'Basically everything.'

The kids love it, though, because almost all Alaskan kids love basketball.

'Something for the bear container,' Fiona says, waving the garbage bag at Lillian.

Lillian covers her nose.

'Yeah, if I were a bear, I'd be all over that.'

Then she goes back to her postcards.

Finn, from Colorado, comes out of the kitchen with a cup of coffee and nods at Fiona. She doesn't trust him, mainly because he's really, really cute in a swoony kind of way, and he knows it. He ties his long hair up in a man bun and wears a headlamp, even though it's light all night and nobody needs a headlamp.

'Habit,' he said when someone asked him about it.

Fiona cannot imagine a scenario where anyone would need to wear a headlamp so often that it became a habit.

What is he, a coal miner? A mole?

He points to the garbage bag. 'Maybe we should hide those pants and map the coordinates, see if the kids can find them with a compass before a bear does.'

'What do you mean, "map the coordinates"?'

The look on his face reminds Fiona that she doesn't fit in the Alaskan brochures Finn and the others read before heading north. Every time she or Amy asks a question, they get the same response, as if being from Alaska means they are supposed to know everything about the outdoors, from dog mushing to kayaking at night to rebuilding the engine of a bush plane.

'Are you kidding?' says Finn. 'I thought Alaskan kids learned how to use a compass in utero.'

'Whoa, there, Mr Know-It-All,' says Lillian suddenly. 'Did you forget to get off your high horse before you tied it up at the barn?'

'Sorry, I'm just surprised,' he says. 'I'm out.' He makes a motion like an umpire at home plate, switches on his unnecessary headlamp, and backs out of the lodge.

'Thanks for that,' says Fiona.

'Don't worry about it. I get enough of that attitude back home. Small towns, you know? Everybody's an expert.'

'Yeah, Alaska's basically just a really big small town. I get it.'

She really should learn to use a compass, though. Fiona adds it to the list of things she didn't know she was supposed to know in order to survive.

'Are you going to do something with that, by the way?' Lillian points at Nick's pants. Fiona can't believe she's still holding the bag.

'Yep, going. I'm out.' She mimics Finn's impression of an ump calling a play and is happy to see Lillian crack a smile.

Are they even worth saving? Is Nick's mom really going to want them back in another week?

Nick and Franky's mom, Nightingale, is a folk singer who is spending her free summer days at festivals without her sons, singing about wagon wheels and things blowing in the wind. Most of the counsellors at Wildwood are of the folk-singing variety. Even Finn was mesmerised by Nightingale's tiny sandalled feet and the way her flowery dress was just see-through enough to accentuate both her hairy legs and the fact that she did not believe in underwear.

But even more noticeable to Fiona was how quickly Nightingale had dropped off her kids. When Fiona mentioned this while on KP duty, the cook, who was thirty, said, 'When you're a parent you can have an opinion, but at seventeen you don't know shit.'

Cook was rummaging through a box of vegetables Nightingale had dropped off when she'd dropped off her boys.

'Would you just take a look at this organic broccoli from her garden.'

Fiona knew a lot about delinquent parents, actually, if anybody cared to ask. Which they didn't.

'Nobody has broccoli growing by mid-June,' she said to Amy as they made their way to the water spigot that night, slapping mosquitoes off each other's cheeks and arms while they walked.

'Maybe Nightingale has a greenhouse.'

Amy held out her brush and Fiona squeezed a dab of Crest onto both their bristles.

'Maybe people just believe what they want to believe,' she said.

Amy pumped the spigot, splashing water on Fiona's sneakers.

'Well, you'd know all about that,' said Amy.

She spat toothpaste into a patch of devil's club.

'What?' said Fiona.

'Nothing, never mind.'

Amy was not acting like herself. She had always let everything roll off her back so easily – this just didn't make sense. Fiona and Amy's friendship had lasted this long because Amy wasn't melodramatic or selfish. Even the day they met, their first day of preschool, Amy had been the one to let Fiona know she had her back.

Amy had been wearing brightly coloured tights with polka dots on them, and Fiona's had been just a muddy brown that she hated. She'd dipped them into the toilet and pretended to cry. When the teachers tried to console her, she'd pointed at Amy's tights and said, 'I wish I had those.'

Amy took off her polka-dotted tights and handed them over, right then and there.

'My Momo put extras in my cubby anyway,' she said. Fiona had been baffled, but also pleased. She'd looked into Amy's wide green eyes, searching for some hidden motive beyond kindness, which in her four short years she had not seen a whole lot of. When you are raised by alcoholics, you learn quickly how to get things in a slanted sort of way but are leery when you succeed.

The day Amy had simply blinked knowingly at Fiona and given her the tights, as if to say 'I don't know why you have to do it this way, but okay,' became something of a pattern as the years went by.

Everything about Amy's life was the opposite of Fiona's. She had a nice Momo who lived with her family and made Amy interesting lunches. Her parents didn't drink too much, and they gave Fiona a curfew if she slept over, just like Amy's. 'We care about you,' Amy's father said. 'We don't want you out wandering the streets at night. We'd never get any sleep.'

Fiona's own family rarely lost any sleep worrying about her. The only person who's even sent her a card here at camp is Amy's Momo. It's in her back pocket now as she makes her way down to the waterfront with Nick's pants. Amy is supposed to be waiting by the bear container with all their campers. The counsellors work in pairs, two for twenty kids, switching every week so nobody is always stuck with the six-year-olds. Fiona is relieved that she didn't get paired up with a counsellor from Outside.

She passes a group of older kids, who appear to be writing letters in the arts and crafts tent. Scattered among them are pictures of bunnies and razors and some other disturbing images that look like indistinguishable bloody blobs. One of the girls is crying; her friend is patting her gently on the shoulders.

'I know it's hard to see,' their counsellor, Maggie, from Pennsylvania, is saying, 'but that's why we have to write and let these companies know we want them to stop testing their products on animals.'

'Hi,' says Fiona. 'What're you guys doing?'

'Letter-writing campaign to razor companies,' Maggie says without looking up.

'Razor companies?'

'Yes. They use bunnies to test their products, and sometimes the animals die in the process.'

'Oh. Wow.'

'My dad hunts rabbits,' says Evan, one of the few kids who are at camp because their parents thought it might actually be fun.

Fiona remembers Amy trying to tell Maggie at orientation that there might be a different standard here, regarding animals and, um, hunting and ... But she'd trailed off when Maggie gave her a bony stare and informed Amy that she was also vegan.

'I like that black lipstick,' Amy had said. 'The colour really suits you.'

'What's a vegan?' Fiona had whispered later as they walked to their cabins.

'No idea,' said Amy, 'but I don't think they eat real food.'

Fiona smiled at Evan now, willing him with her eyes to stop talking.

'And how do you think rabbits feel about being hunted?' Maggie asked him.

Evan looked confused.

'I guess I never thought about it.' He looked at Fiona for help. 'They're kind of overpopulating and they taste good?'

'How would you like it if someone talked about you that way?' Maggie snapped.

Evan blinked and looked even more confused by the idea that he might overpopulate and taste good boiled in a pot.

'That's what we're doing here. We're thinking about poor, defenceless animals and how they *feel*.'

Fiona gave Evan what she hoped was an encouraging smile. Time to get going.

Fireweed lines the trail, but it hasn't yet begun to bloom. Camp won't be over until it's topped off, when the pink flowers turn to white cottony puffs and blow away. Fiona wonders if her energy for this job will top off before the fireweed does, or before the mosquitoes have sucked all the blood from her body.

She stares out at the ice-cold turquoise lake fed by a glacier that hangs between two mountains overlooking camp. From here, the small bodies of the campers look even smaller, splashing around in the blue-green water as if it's a heated pool. One thing about Alaska kids, they are pretty tough. Or maybe they have no idea that not everyone swims in frigid water.

At orientation the counsellors were told to watch the younger swimmers closely and throw them into the sauna to warm up when they start turning blue. She can see that a couple of boys are butt naked, waggling their rear ends at each other and then diving into the freezing lake. Whoever is supposed to be watching them is nowhere around.

A little girl is sitting alone near the water, animatedly clapping and smiling, but not at the boys. She seems to be in her own little world. Every once in a while she jumps up, arms in the air, like a cheerleader. Fiona shields her eyes from the sun, trying to see better. The lake is glassy calm; there's nothing out there. Yet the girl springs into the air again, erupting in applause.

Kids are so weird sometimes.

A quarter mile down the trail, Fiona smells cigarette smoke. Smoking is prohibited in camp, and there's a burn ban in effect. She knows one person who smokes when she's stressed.

'Amy?'

Amy's frizzy blonde mop pops up immediately to Fiona's left.

'Oh no. You smelled it?'

'Are you okay?'

'Our campers are having a boating lesson, not that

159

you asked,' says Amy. 'I needed a break. And I did bring my water bottle to put it out with. I'm not a total idiot.'

Finn has been making everyone fire aware by updating them every day about the wildfire burning near his hometown in Colorado. Fiona was hoping maybe he'd leave early if he was so worried about it. But she figures the updates are a chance for him to hear himself speak, more than anything. Wildfire is one thing he didn't need to brief them on. Alaskans are well versed on the subject. Amy and Fiona are more afraid of fires than they are of bears.

Amy is perched on a rotten log riddled with ants, hidden by fireweed and pushki (which the other counsellors call cow parsnip). Things must be serious if Amy is sitting on ants. Fiona squeezes on next to her, trying not to get pushki sap on her skin. (Also worse than bears are blisters from pushki.)

'I miss the mall,' says Amy. 'Mostly Payless Shoes. I just want to go sniff all that fake leather, put on the little nylon footies, and try on some pumps that I can't afford.'

'I know,' says Fiona. Even though Amy's just talking about shoes, she's starting to sound a little less edgy.

'I want to tell you something before you do anything to ruin it,' she says.

Okay, that was edgy.

'I have a crush on Finn.'

Ew, gross.

'What would I do to ruin it?'

'Oh, I don't know, Fiona. Act like he's not good enough for me, as if you're just being a good friend?'

'Excuse me?'

'When are you going to admit how you lost us our jobs?'

'I reported a guy who jumped out of the walk-in cooler, spraying you with whipped cream through a foot-long hot dog. Did you forget?'

'You weren't even there, Fiona, remember? You called in sick?'

'Yeah, but I was sticking up for you, Amy. I reported it when you told me it happened.'

'It was just a stupid prank. Who cares?'

'He's a pervert. He was always doing shit like that. You also don't think it's weird that we lost our jobs and he didn't?'

'His brother was the manager. Of course he wasn't going to lose his job.'

Fiona can't believe Amy is shooting the messenger like this.

'You called in sick when you weren't sick, so yes, you should have lost your job,' Amy says. 'And I lost mine because I covered for your lie. And not for the first time,' she adds.

She lights another cigarette.

'Shhh ...' says Fiona.

'Oh, right. Don't talk, Amy, just let it roll off like you always do,' she says sarcastically.

'No, I mean, do you hear that?'

The thump of many pairs of hiking boots is suddenly very close. And then they hear Maggie saying, 'Okay, everyone ready? A one and a two and a ...'

Ten campers begin to chant, 'MAKE CAMP FANTASTIC, DON'T WASTE PLASTIC!' over and over and over and over.

They must be done writing their letters to the razor companies.

Now Maggie's group has transformed into a litter brigade. Cleaning up the trails, picking up wrappers and plastic bags, waving signs as they merrily march along. 'Don't waste plastic' slogans are painted onto greasy pizza boxes taped to willow branches, bobbing in the air.

Maggie's nose suddenly wrinkles and she holds up a hand, silencing her campers. They halt, so close Fiona could reach out and touch the toe of Maggie's purple sandal.

Amy is holding a soggy cigarette butt as if it's a murder weapon and she's been framed.

Maggie's face appears between the pushki, like a disembodied head.

'Howdy,' says Fiona. She's never used that word

before, but that's what happens when you're hiding on a log like a fugitive. You just don't sound like yourself.

'What are you two *doing* in there?'

'We heard your, um, campaign, is it? And we were looking for litter,' says Fiona. 'Because our campers are out boating right now and we had some free time.'

Maggie looks suspicious, but also pleased that maybe she's getting through to them.

'And we found this!'

Fiona grabs the cigarette butt out of Amy's hand and jams it into Maggie's face.

'I *know*. Can you believe it?' she says as Maggie recoils. 'We need to have an all-camp meeting and make sure nobody is smoking. For their safety and the safety of everyone here.'

Amy stares at Fiona as if she's grown a horn.

'Totally,' says Maggie. 'Can you imagine if someone started a wildfire?'

'I shudder to even think,' says Fiona, trying to keep a straight face.

Evan, who seems to want to make up for hunting rabbits, jumps in with another witty slogan:

'DON'T SMOKE, IT'S NO JOKE. DON'T SMOKE, IT'S NO JOKE.'

His fellow campers join him.

'We should go collect our kids from their boating lesson,' says Amy. She tugs Fiona's arm.

Her fingernails are digging into Fiona's skin a little harder than necessary.

'That right there is what I'm talking about,' says Amy, once they are far enough away that she can whisper-yell in Fiona's face. 'You're a professional liar.'

'What? I just saved your ass, in case you didn't notice.'

'Oh, this again! You're delusional if you think you're the saviour, Fiona.'

'Why are you so mad? I already said I was sorry that you vouched for me.'

'Where were you when you called in sick?'

'I was …'

'You went to the movies with Mason Hawk.'

'How did you … know that?'

'Does it matter? You knew I liked him, Fiona. I cover for you and you pay me back by sneaking off behind my back.'

'I didn't tell you because he asked me not to.'

Amy's cheeks are the shade of ripe plums.

'I'm so tired of this.'

'What? Wait. Let me talk.'

But Amy walks off toward the lake mumbling about how much she hates this place and how she is *never, ever going to have kids, not in a million years.*

Three little girls in pink frilly swimsuits see her at just that moment and screech, 'Amyyyyyy! We picked you these flowers!'

They run to her with bouquets of invasive weeds and she throws her arms around them, exclaiming wildly, 'These are so beautiful! Let's see if we can find something for a vase. You three have made my day.'

Fiona watches thoughtfully for a few minutes as her friend who hates children swoons over the bouquet. It was so out of character for Amy to yell at her like that. But maybe Amy doesn't want to be the duck that always lets all the water roll off her back. Fiona should have noticed sooner, because the only person who has ever trusted her doesn't seem to trust her anymore.

Oh shit, where are Nick's pants? She can't remember where she last had them.

The little girl who was cheerleading for nobody is still sitting on a rock by the water, but now she's talking to herself, holding her towel off to the side and having a conversation with the empty space beside her.

Fiona goes over and kneels down in front of her.

'Hey there,' she says.

'Hi,' says the girl. She stops talking but is looking to her left, smiling at the empty air.

'Whatcha doin'?'

'Helping Elizabeth dry off.'

'Oh. Who's Elizabeth?'

'She's my friend. She's a mermaid. She just got out of the water.'

'Were you cheering her on while she swam?'

The girl looks Fiona in the eye. Is that relief on her face?

'Uh-huh. Can you see her too?'

'Um, sure. Hi, Elizabeth.' Fiona pretends to shake hands with absolutely nothing.

The girl giggles.

'You're just moving her tail up and down.'

'Well, that's because I thought that's how mermaids say hello.'

'She has hands, silly!'

'Of course. Sorry, Elizabeth. Let's shake hands.'

Apparently she does it right the second time, because the girl looks pleased.

'I'm Fiona.' She holds out her hand again.

'I'm Poppy.' Poppy takes Fiona's fingers and gives them a shake.

'Where's the rest of your group, Poppy?'

But chatty Poppy suddenly turns quiet and shy.

'Hey, you okay? Did you lose your group?'

Poppy shakes her head.

'Do you know who your counsellor is?'

Poppy nods.

Wow. Why the abrupt change?

Finn comes out of the sauna in a pair of baggy swim trunks, his tanned arms and legs very visible. His elbows are propped high on the door as he leans over someone standing against it. He bends down to whisper something into her ear, and Fiona sees that it's Amy, holding the invasive weeds against her chest, tilting her ear up to hear.

'That's him,' says Poppy. 'That's my counsellor.'

'Poppy, are you scared of him?'

She shakes her head but whispers, 'Elizabeth is, though.'

More of Amy and Fiona's campers are swarming the beach, wet from their boating lesson.

'Fiona,' says a nasal voice near her elbow, 'I already have a backpack, so I don't need to borrow gear for the campout.'

She looks into Andrew's round, pudgy face. His nostrils are coated in crusted snot that looks a lot like dried glue. How does he breathe?

'You have a way to carry your sleeping bag and parts of the tent? You're sure?'

'Yes, I brought my own backpack from home.'

'Okay, because you guys have to all share the weight between the four of you in your group.'

He rolls his eyes. 'I know, I know, Fiona. I'm staying here longer than anyone. My mom told me what to bring.'

She remembers that Andrew is here for a month, even though a week is too long for most of the campers his age. Fiona thinks the money would have been better spent on his adenoids, but then she remembers

Cook telling her she's too young to have opinions: 'Save it for when you're a parent.'

Yeah, that's not happening, she thinks.

'Okay, Andrew, you don't have to come to gear checkout. Go have fun with your, uh, friends.'

Does Andrew have any friends?

When she turns back around, Poppy and Elizabeth are gone.

Later, at the gear shed, Amy is still barely talking to Fiona, but there's no time anyway. It's total chaos trying to sort gear for twenty kids. They dole out internal frame packs, tents, and sleeping bags as if they know exactly what they're doing. For their group, it's mostly symbolic: they are going to walk less than five hundred feet from their cabins and pitch tents on top of a grassy hill they could practically reach with a long stick.

For six-year-olds it's just a chance to work as a group and get the *idea* of hiking and sleeping out. Amy and Fiona have never camped in their lives, but since no one asked, they pretend they were born doing this.

Amy has a clipboard with everyone's names on it. They are pulling out tent poles and rainflies, and she tells them to split all the pieces up and see if they can carry them in their packs. Eventually, and after a great deal of confusion, they are surrounded by kids who look like they've been impaled by tent poles sticking out at all angles. Now they just need to walk up that hill, easy peasy.

'Hey, Franky, when Andrew gets here with his pack, give him part of the tent to carry. And a sleeping bag, okay?'

'He's sleeping in our tent? But he snores like a snow machine!'

'Be *nice*,' says Fiona. 'I'm going to the mess hall to get the s'mores and hot dogs and stuff. I'll be right back.'

'That's what you said last time,' says Amy, but she's busy trying to get her girls to stop using the rainfly as a parachute. 'Okay, everybody out,' she says as she trips and falls into the middle of it.

'A big fat fly!' cries one of the girls.

'Let's eat her for lunch!' Six other very dirty spiders in wet pink bathing suits fall on top of Amy.

Fiona slips away.

But she has one quick stop before the mess hall.

'This is a pretty serious accusation,' the director says when Fiona tells her her concerns. 'Do you have any proof?'

'I'm not saying Finn did anything. I'm just saying that little girl, Poppy, seemed genuinely scared of him.'

'You don't seem to be making a lot of friends among the counsellors, Fiona.'

'I swear this isn't about me.'

'Well, I think Finn deserves to know what he's

being accused of,' she says. 'And don't you have campers you should be attending to right now?'

Why does everyone shoot the messenger?

'Can I just look at Poppy's intake sheet? The one her parents filled out?'

'Why? Usually just the camper's counsellor gets to do that.'

'We do sometimes have to help out other people's campers. If there's something in there we should all know so we don't do the wrong thing, I'd like to read it.'

'Since you seem so concerned about this girl, fine. You can look at her sheet.'

'Great.'

'After your campout. You have a job to do right now.'

'Can I at least bring a copy to read once my kids are asleep?'

She can tell the director doesn't like her. It's not as if Fiona fell off the turnip truck yesterday, as her father used to say. He was usually three sheets to the wind when he said it, though.

The director hands her Poppy's intake sheet. 'Get back to your campers.'

'Thank you for caring SO MUCH about children,' Fiona says, but only inside her head.

Back at the gear shed, Andrew is holding a tiny Snoopy backpack in front of his face, fending off three other boys who are crowding around him, waving tent poles as if they are billy clubs. His backpack is big enough to hold maybe half a peanut butter sandwich and an apple.

'Andrew, is that the backpack you told me you brought from home?'

'Fiona, the others have already made him aware that it's too small,' Amy says, a note of warning in her voice.

'Jesus Christ,' says Fiona, 'I said over and over that he had to carry a tent and a sleeping bag and he kept saying he had it covered. A tiny Snoopy backpack is his idea of having it covered?'

'Why is everyone here so mean?' yells Andrew, throwing Snoopy down and crashing off into the bushes like a baby moose.

'Way to go,' Amy says.

'Do you want to go after him?'

'No, it's better if you make it right,' she says, 'even though I'm beginning to wonder if this was your plan all along, always leaving me with ninety percent of our group.'

'I'll bring him right back. Ten minutes, tops. I promise.'

But Fiona cannot find Andrew. After the ten minutes are up, there's still no Andrew. Has any counsellor in the history of Camp Wildwood ever lost a camper before?

'Andrewwwwwwwww. Come out. You're missing s'moooorrrres.'

She's about to call it quits and head back to admit to the director that it isn't Finn they should be worried about, but her. She is the worst possible person to be put in charge of children. She'll turn herself in.

But then a flash of red curled up under a scrubby spruce tree catches her eye.

By the time she reaches him, her arms and cheeks are scraped from squeezing through dead, clawing branches. Fiona scrunches up her arms and legs, trying not to touch him.

She says nothing, tired of words, tired of always doing the wrong thing, even when she tries so hard to do the right thing, whatever the hell that is.

They each sit hunched in a round ball of silence, except for Andrew's sporadic sobbing and adenoidal wheezing. From the corner of her eye she sees dead mosquitoes in his hair, blood and bites on his cheek. How will he survive till the end of camp? How will she?

'I'm so sorry,' Fiona says. 'I didn't mean to make you feel bad.'

She is thinking about Amy. How coming from a family that buys you nice tights and cuts your sandwiches into cute shapes and remembers to pick you up from preschool is such a simple, beautiful thing.

It does not prepare a person for how scary the world really is.

But Fiona knows. And Andrew knows. And Poppy seems to know, or at least, her invisible friend, Elizabeth, does.

'Why did you have to go and make such a big deal about my tiny backpack in front of everyone?' says Andrew.

'I know. I'm sorry. What can I say to make it better, Andrew?'

'Nothing,' he says.

Truer words were never spoken.

But his shoulders have stopped shaking. His red, puffy eyes look up at her with a glint in them so deep, she knows he's going to spout something profound that will save them both.

'Have you ever seen that movie *Escape to Witch Mountain*?'

'Um, no. Actually, I haven't.'

And then he proceeds to tell her the whole movie, in exquisite detail. She realises Amy is going to genuinely kill her. But she owes him this. He's probably never had anyone give him this much attention in his life.

An hour later they make it back to camp. Amy's clothes and face look like she's been in the trenches of World War I. Her ponytail is coming out of its scrunchie, and there's marshmallow in her hair. But all the tents are up, and nineteen very sticky campers are happily roasting hot dogs over a blazing fire. She should win counsellor of the year, Fiona thinks. She didn't know Amy even knew how to make a fire.

'I'm sorry,' she says, and Amy waves her away with the willow branch she's whittling into a point.

'Don't make me stab you with this,' she says without looking up. 'It's very sharp.' There's a long, long pause before she adds, 'Andrew looks absolutely transformed. What did you do?'

'Kind of nothing,' Fiona says, which is a lie and the truth.

The kids have moved on from hot dogs and are now thrusting flaming marshmallows at her, asking for chocolate and graham crackers.

Fiona doles out s'more fixings. Then she looks at Amy and says, 'Did I ever tell you what happened the day you gave me your tights in preschool?'

'I actually hated those tights,' says Amy. 'It wasn't that big of a deal, Fiona.'

'Yeah, it was,' Fiona says, 'I got left at preschool that day. Nobody came to pick me up.'

'What do you mean?'

'My mom just forgot about me. I remember sitting at the colouring table and seeing the sky outside getting darker and darker and hearing Ms Everett call someone, whispering that she didn't know what to do.

I knew she was talking about me. Remember those homemade worksheets she made about Dog and Moose and Bear going sledding together? I just pretended to colour the same moose on a toboggan over and over again.'

The marshmallows are all gone, but Fiona keeps unwrapping pieces of Hershey's chocolate and stacking them onto graham crackers anyway, as if in a trance.

'Someone came, I can't remember who. It could have been a policeman, or the owner of the preschool, or a social worker. I got moved around for days between different strangers' houses. I still had your tights, which was the only thing I had that was supposedly my own, even if they weren't really mine.'

'That's so crazy,' says Amy. 'I had no idea. Why have you never said anything?'

'I guess I was embarrassed.'

Amy nods.

'Maybe you were right. Maybe I really do want things because they're yours.'

'Really?'

'Not Mason Hawk, I swear. But you know, a nice grandmother from Denmark, like your Momo. Or just the fact that people worry about you if you don't come home at night. I want all those things.'

'My family loves you.'

'Yeah, but they're still yours.'

They watch their campers lazily yawning next to the fire, mesmerised by the flames. Fiona doesn't remember ever feeling that content when she was six.

'Someone told me they saw you and Mason together that night,' Amy says quietly.

'So why didn't you say anything before now?'

'I guess I was embarrassed too. And also jealous and hurt.'

Fiona understands being embarrassed. But Amy really didn't need to be jealous or hurt.

'He just wanted to ask me about you. He told me not to say anything, but that's all I was doing with him, answering questions about you. But then we got fired and you were so mad ... I honestly forgot about it.'

'Oh my God,' Amy puts her face in her hands. 'Fiona, I really thought ...'

'Yeah, I know.'

She remembers the camp director's squinty eyes. *You don't seem to be making a lot of friends among the counsellors, Fiona.*

'I really jumped to the worst conclusion, didn't I?' says Amy.

Andrew has crawled into Fiona's lap, covered in ketchup and snot and mosquito blood, and fallen asleep. He's already snoring.

'It's just hard, you know,' Amy says. 'Believing you sometimes. I wish it wasn't like that.'

'I want us to be friends in fifty years,' says Fiona. 'How do we make sure that happens?'

'Well, for starters, I can't just let everything roll off me anymore.'

'Yeah, I noticed that too.'

'And you have to trust me.'

It's true; Fiona trusts barely anyone. But Amy isn't just anyone.

'I will try harder, I promise.'

Another thing she's always liked about Amy is that she knows when to stop talking.

'Come on, let's get these guys in their tents,' says Amy.

In the firelight, their campers have just fallen asleep wherever they've landed. Some still hold charred willow sticks in their grubby fists, their bodies and faces covered in so many layers of food and dirt and dead bugs, they may need archaeologists to come in and dig them out to find their real skin.

Amy and Fiona nudge their little Jell-O bodies, trying to get them to walk, then finally give up and carry the ones that have collapsed.

'It's solstice tonight,' Amy says.

'Is it?' asks Fiona as she picks up a groggy camper still wearing a sandy pink swimsuit. Do these girls even have any real clothes?

'The other counsellors are having some kind of celebration. Finn told me to meet him by the lake.'

'I thought we only did that in the winter?' whispers Fiona. 'You know, when the sun comes back. Who wants to celebrate shorter days ahead?'

'I guess people do it because it's the longest day of the year,' Amy says. 'Just another thing we didn't get the memo about.' She holds up a melted shoe that was too close to the fire.

'Yeah, I bet everyone thinks Alaska was wasted on us,' says Fiona.

'Maybe, but I might go down and celebrate, if you don't mind. Payback for doing all the setup?' She holds her hands together as if in prayer and blinks rapidly at Fiona. 'Please?'

'Sure, of course. Have fun.'

Fiona needs to read Poppy's intake sheet before she says anything about Finn. Even though Amy just said they should be honest, if Fiona accuses Finn and is wrong, it will be the last straw for her and Amy.

But her gut tells her she's not wrong.

She carries Andrew to his tent and puts him down next to his Snoopy backpack. Nick and Franky stare at her in disbelief as Andrew's snores rev into gear. Fiona laughs and whispers, *'Aw, c'mon, you guys. Give him a break.'*

They cover their ears with sweatshirts and pillows, then curl up together and slowly fall asleep beneath the midnight sun.

After Amy goes to meet Finn and the others, Fiona sits alone at the fire, holding Poppy's information. For a second, she thinks about just tossing it into the flames – why stir the pot? But then she hears Poppy's voice saying she's not scared, but 'Elizabeth is, though.'

She opens Poppy's intake sheet and reads.

What do you hope your child will gain from camp? *Poppy suffered a traumatic loss when her best friend went missing and was never found. They were both six at the time. She's been doing much better since we moved to Alaska, and we hope she'll make some friends her own age at Camp Wildwood.*

Any concerns that we should know about? *For quite a while after the loss of her friend, Poppy developed an intense relationship with an invisible friend she called Elizabeth. She's eight now, and too old for invisible friends – we hope. For the past six months, she seems to have moved on and no longer needs Elizabeth quite as much. If Elizabeth were to surface again at camp, it would signal that Poppy may have had some kind of relapse, and we would appreciate being contacted immediately.*

Even if Finn had done nothing to make Poppy afraid, he was supposed to have read the intake sheet. Shouldn't he have let her family know that Elizabeth is back?

'Fiona! Come quick! Nick was peeing and then something shot out of his butt! Hurry!'

She must have fallen asleep by the fire.

Oh, Nick, no, no, no. No. Please. Not again.

Franky and Andrew are hiding behind a tree, watching Nick, whose pants are down around his ankles.

There's also a bear about fifty yards away on the trail, sniffing, nose in the air.

Fiona cannot breathe. Or move. She tries willing Nick with her mind to just step out of his pants, leave them on the ground, and back away slowly. But Nick hasn't seen the bear yet.

'Franky, get me some leaves!' he shouts.

'No, Franky, stay put,' Fiona says.

'Why?'

Fiona points. Franky freaks out. 'A bear! A bear! Go away, bear! Go away, bear!' He's waving his arms and jumping up and down, which is exactly what you're supposed to do when you see a bear. Fiona forgot this important information from orientation.

'Good job, Franky!'

Now Andrew has joined in, and Nick has stepped out of his pants and is jumping up and down with a bare bum. They are all yelling and making themselves big, which, compared with a huge brown bear, doesn't mean all that much.

'Okay, but back away, guys,' Fiona says. 'Slowly. Back away slowly.'

At the last second she thinks to snag Nick's pants with a long stick and toss them as far as she can in the bear's direction. That should keep him (or her) busy.

'I don't have any more pants,' Nick says, but he backs away like Fiona told him to.

'You can have a pair of mine,' says Andrew.

'Okay, yeah,' says Fiona, eyes on the bear. 'You can wear Andrew's.'

Suddenly the bear's ears prick up and it turns to look over its shoulder. Fiona follows the bear's gaze . . .

Oh shit!

Poppy is walking along the trail in her nightgown and slippers. What is she doing out of bed?

'Oh my God, oh my God, oh my God.' Fiona grabs a metal pot and a spatula. She bangs wildly on the pot to get the bear's attention.

'Come get these jeans!' she yells. 'Yummy, yummy!'

Franky, Nick, and Andrew look at each other questioningly. Yummy?

Poppy hears the banging and stops. The bear freezes too, confused by all the noise; it just stands in the trail, halfway between Poppy and Fiona.

The rest of the camp hears the noise. Lillian runs

over, banging a huge cowbell with a stick. Everyone is making as much noise as they can, until the bear looks so confused it heads off in the only direction where no humans are yelling and screaming.

Fiona drops the spatula and the pot, rushes to Poppy, and hugs her hard.

'What are you doing out of bed, Poppy?'

'I was looking for Finn.'

'I'm right here,' says a voice behind Fiona. 'I'm sorry, Poppy. I'm here.'

He picks her up and holds her tight.

'I can't find Elizabeth.'

Fiona is totally baffled. Isn't Elizabeth scared of Finn?

'What's going on?' Amy must have arrived with him.

'Poppy is from my hometown,' Finn says. 'When her mom found out I was working here, she requested me as Poppy's counsellor.'

'But Elizabeth is scared of you,' Fiona blurts out.

'Her name is Poppy, Fiona,' Amy whispers. 'And she doesn't look scared.'

No time to fill her in.

Poppy is relaxed in Finn's arms. She even giggles. 'Fiona shook Elizabeth's tail.'

Finn's face grows serious. 'Poppy?' he says. 'Did you need to see Elizabeth? Is that why she was here?'

'She was only here for the day.'

'Poppy, why was Elizabeth scared of Finn?' Fiona asks.

'I'll tell you why,' says Finn, not at all surprised by the question. 'Because Elizabeth knows she's not signed up for camp. Right, Poppy? I can see her with my special invisible mermaid headlamp. She knows I have to call Poppy's mom if she shows up.'

Fiona just stares at him. Special invisible mermaid headlamp?

'Nobody is mad at you or Elizabeth,' Finn tells Poppy. 'But I should still call your mom.'

'Elizabeth really wanted to swim in the lake and splash her tail around,' says Poppy. 'She knows I don't need her anymore, but sometimes she still needs me.'

Poppy rests her head against Finn's shoulder and closes her eyes. 'I want my mom anyway.'

Fiona is so relieved that she never told Amy her suspicions. So relieved that the camp director didn't take her seriously. Best of all, nobody got eaten by a bear tonight.

Although, unbeknownst to any of them, down by the mud pits, a brown bear is ripping Nick's other pair of soiled, forgotten pants into smithereens.

The Stranger in the Woods

The summer the wildfire ripped through the forest and then licked dangerously at the houses on the edge of town was the summer Jenny learned that fire might actually be her friend.

She hadn't really paid attention in school when they'd studied ecosystems and how wildfires were the age-old way that the earth took care of itself, since long before the arrival of humans. Her high school had added a new subject, ecology, taught by a very young graduate of the University of Colorado, who had stressed that lightning strikes were necessary: they ignited and burned old growth, thus making way for new growth. Circle of life. Birth, rebirth. The best way to fight fire was with fire. Blah, blah, blah. Why did they need to learn this?

Now, Jenny was surprised to realise that some of it had actually sunk in. During that fateful summer when the wildfire smoke had scorched their lungs every single day and practically the whole town had had to evacuate, Jenny had been consoled by one important thing she'd learned in that class: 'Fire is essential for managing the forest. It keeps the ecosystem healthy without interference from man.'

In the margin of her notes, Jenny had written 'or woman', and punctuated it with a smiley face, figuring her young, hip teacher would appreciate the sentiment. Besides, she'd thought, she would never need to know this stuff in real life. The class had mainly been an exercise in equality and the evolution of language, or so she'd thought.

But now, as the woods near her house continued to burn and the winds took a nasty turn, the Forest Service announced a level three evacuation order, and everyone had to scramble to leave their homes, grabbing whatever valuables they could at the last second.

People had built way too close to the forest, and Mother Nature didn't really give a damn about things like subdivisions or the skyrocketing price of insurance. The fire had started more than a hundred miles away, outside Granville, but warm weather and drought had brought the flames right to Jenny's doorstep.

Before this summer, the only threat in that thick stand of dead spruce near her house had happened ten years ago. It wasn't fire, but a stranger who had emerged from those trees and threatened their safety. Jenny was so sick of hearing that particular story, she was almost relieved to see it being rewritten by nature.

Not Jenny but her sister, Jade, had been riding her bike near the dead-end road that abutted the forest. Jade had been about six, and had just gotten her training wheels off. Seven-year-old Jenny hadn't been there, but she could imagine it: her younger sister, standing up on her pedals and braking with the full force of her weight, scattering pebbles beneath her tyres.

Jade had always been overly sure of herself, in Jenny's opinion.

The part about the man coming out of the woods was harder for Jenny's brain to wrap itself around, since she and her sister never really saw strangers. They lived in a place where everyone knew everyone. Jenny knew about strangers, of course, but the girls had never been anywhere that they might run into one, except for maybe JC Penney. It was the only place they could even imagine wandering off and getting separated from their mother. The one place where their mother had bothered to use that delicious word – 'stranger' – which always made Jade and Jenny move a little closer to the hem of her skirt, as if she were base in a game of tag.

But in their neighbourhood, mountain lions were a bigger threat than strangers. Also rare, but they had at least been spotted once or twice. 'Strangers', though: that was an exotic, spine-tingling word.

So Jenny had been especially jealous when Jade had met one.

Jade had relished telling the story, how he'd come toward her slowly, with a five-dollar bill in his outstretched hand.

'Here you go, sweetheart,' he'd said. Jade had said he smelled like skunk, and she'd seen a rip in his jeans. Every time her little sister told it, Jenny noticed that the story grew, until it included every missing button on his shirt, the ominous dirt under his fingernails. She doubted very much that Jade was remembering new details for every retelling, but Jenny said nothing, just chewed the inside of her cheek, feeling invisible, while her little sister awed everyone in her typical way.

Jade had taken the money and then whipped away on her bike (her words again), standing expertly on her pedals. Jenny knew that Jade thought the people she was telling the story to would be impressed by this.

Jade loved an audience.

'Hold on there, darling,' the man had said. 'There's lots more money where that came from, if you just come through these trees with me.'

Even back then, Jenny had been sceptical of the words 'darling' and 'sweetheart' coming out of her sister's mouth in a drawl she'd never heard before, but the five dollars was certainly real. For weeks, Jade had had her eye on a yellow raincoat at JC Penney, one that came with a matching umbrella – also yellow, with pictures of more umbrellas on it – and she just needed five more dollars to add to her birthday money before she could afford it.

'That's okay,' she'd called over her shoulder to the man. 'This is just enough. Thanks!'

Over time, people had even joked about this last bit, how if Jade had been just a little greedier, she might not be around to tell the story. Jenny had never thought the joking was funny, especially because the man was never found, and a tiny part of her thought maybe Jade had lied just to make herself seem even more interesting.

It seemed that people had forgotten about the stranger in the woods until two years ago, when another six-year-old girl went missing, in another part of the state. She still hadn't been found. Jenny was conflicted, since she had always doubted Jade's story, just a little bit. After all this time, could the same stranger still be out there, calling little girls 'darling' with a drawl like a country singer and luring them with money? She couldn't believe that she'd actually been jealous of Jade and that stupid umbrella.

As the fire bore down on them, they'd had to leave their cat, Colonel Mustard, because they couldn't find him. Jenny was frantic. He was mostly hers, and she thought he might be hiding on the top shelf of her closet, but the fire crew had refused to let them go back. One of them had even grabbed her arm to stop her from running inside. Under his hard hat, his face was covered with soot, making the whites of his eyes stand out.

'You can't go in there,' he said, his fingers leaving a black ring around her forearm.

'My cat ...' she whispered, and at that moment there was a deafening crash of burning tree limbs falling nearby.

He'd shoved her into the backseat of the car even as she held on to the reflective tape on his jacket.

'Colonel Mustard. His name is Colonel Mustard.'

'I hear you, Miss Scarlett,' he said, and she thought maybe he even smiled.

But as they drove off, she'd heard another crash of burning tree limbs and wondered why people made jokes in the midst of tragedies, and what if she never saw Colonel Mustard again?

That was already a week ago.

Jenny was lying on the makeshift cot in the emergency shelter, eating a bologna sandwich from the Salvation Army and reading an old *People* magazine from a stack that had been donated.

Jade refused to lie down, saying she wasn't going to get bedbugs just because she was now an evacuee.

'I think lice is more of a problem in shelters,' Jenny said casually, noticing that the magazine's pages were stuck together with what looked like grape jelly. She hoped it was grape jelly.

'You girls could make yourselves useful helping with the younger kids,' their mother had said. 'Go read them books or something.'

Jenny and her sister had exchanged a look, and Jade shook her head emphatically, mouthing *head lice* behind her mother's back, which made Jenny laugh and feel for two seconds like they were conspirators. But then Jade's friends Shelby and Carly bounced over, each threading an arm through one of Jade's, announcing that they were heading over to the fire update briefing.

How Jade could have such mindless friends was another mystery that Jenny spent too much time pondering. She watched the threesome giggle and weave drunkenly through all the cots at the shelter, which was really their high school gym. The briefing was still an hour away. As if nobody knew the girls were trying to position themselves front and centre so the incident command officer who led the updates would notice them. He was almost thirty! What would an old guy like that see in a bunch of teenagers who smelled like pomegranate shampoo? This was a disaster, not a prom.

Their family was in danger of losing their home, and still Jade and her friends were acting as if it were merely a chance for them to attract attention. But why would they stop being themselves just because of a fire? *Good riddance*, Jenny thought as they pranced out of the gym.

There'd been an announcement that residents could go back home during a one-hour window to get things they'd left behind. Jenny wanted to go. She remembered the firefighter's grip on her arm.

'Can I come with you and look for Colonel Mustard, Dad?'

'Oh, honey, I don't know if it's safe,' said her mom.

'Well, if they're letting residents in, it can't be too dangerous,' said her dad. 'There must have been a change in the wind or something.'

'So I can come?'

Her mother's right eye twitched, a sign that she was anxious. 'Why don't we wait for them to go back to level two. Then at least we'll know it's safe.'

Jenny thought the Forest Service's system for letting people know when to leave was kind of bogus anyway. They had gone from level one (ready) to level three (go!) in less than two hours, thanks to the wind.

When she and Jade were little, the word 'stranger' was their mother's label for everyone she did not trust. But as they got older, they learned there were categories and subcategories to the strangers their mother held at arm's length. At the moment, she was very distrustful of the Bureau of Land Management. She wanted to wait until Coyote Jones said it was safe, because he was a local and she had more faith in him than she did in 'some bureaucratic arm of the government'. Coyote Jones had been telling people for days to be ready: 'Don't forget the three Ps, everyone: people, pets, papers.'

'Honestly, hon,' her father said, 'if it wasn't safe, they wouldn't let any of us go back in. The cat must be scared out of its wits by now too.' Jenny nodded vehemently.

'Animals are really good at finding safe places to hide,' said her mother. 'I doubt he'll come out until this is all over.'

But Jenny jumped up before her father could be swayed by her mother's eye twitch, which was ramping up.

'We're at level one, Mr Scaife,' she said in what she hoped was her best impression of the fire service spokesperson. She grabbed his arm. 'Level two, Mr Scaife. Get set.

'See you in an hour, Mom. Mr Scaife, we are at level three. Go, go, go!'

That was about as silly as Jenny would get, especially once they were near their neighbourhood. It felt like driving into the apocalypse. Miles of hoses crisscrossed the empty streets, and there were huge holding tanks around the perimeter of every structure. Water trucks were going in and out, filling the tanks, which looked like gigantic blow-up swimming pools. Before they could actually drive down their street, they had to stop at a security checkpoint.

'Yikes, this looks serious,' said her father.

'I just need to see some ID,' said the man at the checkpoint. 'You'd be surprised how much looting there is in a disaster.'

'Really?' said Jenny's father, genuinely surprised. He had a hard time thinking the worst of people, unlike her mother, and in spite of everything they had been through. Jenny often felt like a ping-pong ball bouncing between her parents. They had such different outlooks.

'Yeah, but we also need to know when people come in and out so we don't lose anybody.' The man winked at Jenny.

There was tobacco juice in his beard and a wad of chew in his cheek.

She waited for her father to say something like 'Winking's not really appropriate, don't you think?' Her mother would have. But she knew he was overwhelmed with the idea of looters, and from dealing with the fire, the threat of losing their home. In his mind, if the guy had helped save their home, well, let him wink at Jenny if he wanted to. It was harmless. She bit her cheek and said nothing.

The checkpoint man taped a pass on the windshield

with the date and time, and they drove slowly through the war zone that had once been their neighbourhood. So far, none of the houses had been lost – although two sheds and a chicken coop had burned to the ground and were still smouldering.

There was a big orange X painted on the front door of their house, meaning it had been checked and all residents had evacuated. *All except poor Colonel Mustard*, thought Jenny, turning the knob, which was warm to the touch. Inside, the house smelled like its contents had been broiled with a blow torch. Jenny covered her nose, taking shallow breaths while making the clucking noise that Colonel Mustard liked.

'Here, boy. Who's the precious kitty? C'mon, boy.'

Nothing.

She rummaged under all the beds and in all the closets, although the only closet he ever slept in was hers. When she looked in her sister's closet she was surprised to see the tiny umbrella Jade had bought with the stranger's money stashed in the corner. Why did Jade still have it? Why did her parents – especially her mother? – let her keep money that could have easily led to something sinister?

Why was she just now wondering this?

'Any sign of him?' said her father, sticking his head in the door.

'Nope, just this.' She held up the stupid umbrella.

'That probably won't do much against the fire,' said her dad.

'Why does everyone think it's okay to make jokes?' Jenny tried to keep her voice down but failed. 'You know, you almost lost your daughter to a psychopath.'

She had never said that out loud before. Her father instantly looked hurt.

'Sorry, Jenny. Would you rather we just focus on all the ways we've barely managed to escape tragedy?'

'No, that's not what I meant. Forget it,' she said, throwing the umbrella back into the closet. 'Let's just find Colonel Mustard.'

He was nowhere. Outside, fire crews were spraying down all the houses, keeping them wet. Jenny got up the nerve to ask someone if he'd seen a cat with a broken tail. She was disappointed that it wasn't the same guy who had grabbed her arm when they'd evacuated and then was taken aback by her own disappointment.

'Are you Miss Scarlett?' he asked her, flashing a mouthful of overlapping teeth.

'Excuse me?'

'Nate said if you came back to let you know.'

'Nate?'

'He found your cat. Relish or Ketchup or something?'

'He found Colonel Mustard?'

'Ah, that's it. He was getting off a sixteen-hour shift, so he said he'd take your cat to the shelter.'

'Oh, that's great. That's wonderful. Thank you. Thanks.' She didn't know what else to say and was afraid she'd start bawling with relief. So she extended a hand, which he looked at sceptically. He held up a glove covered in black smudge that appeared to be smoking.

'High five from afar. Glad your cat is okay. You know, except the tail, I guess.'

Then he shouldered a chainsaw and moved past her, toward the crackling fire in the forest beyond.

Her father was quiet all the way back to the high school. Jenny was sick of calling it a shelter: it was a high school, with cots laid out in the gym underneath banners proclaiming their team's cross country and volleyball state titles. The evacuees were all showering in the locker rooms, where the girls usually refused to get naked in front of their classmates and now had to shower with the whole town.

Jenny had pointed this out to Jade, who said, 'That's what a disaster will do,' as if she were an expert on the matter. 'Provide a whole new perspective.'

Right, Jenny had thought, *because the worldly one is so wise.* But of course, she said nothing. Just chewed on her cheek again, the familiar taste of blood reminding her that perspective was something she had a hard time holding on to around Jade.

'Now,' her father said, 'before you go look for Colonel Mustard, you might want to shower. I think we both smell a bit smoky. It might unnerve him.'

'I really want to see him first,' said Jenny. 'I'll shower right after, I promise.'

But when she found him, Colonel Mustard was so freaked out, Jenny realised it had been a mistake to say hi and then leave right away. His broken tail was smudged black on the end, and he wouldn't come out from under the blanket in his crate. There were so many dog carriers filled with stray pets – one even held a ferret – that Jenny worried her cat might have been happier wherever he'd been hiding before he got rescued.

'It's okay, buddy. You're safe now. I'll be right back.'

Because the fire crews also showered at the school, Jenny's father said the men's locker room smelled like hundreds of blackened hot dogs. As Jenny walked to the women's side, wrapped in her towel, she noticed a woman who had just emerged from a shower stall and was towelling off a blue and green tattoo of a dragon across her left butt cheek. When she pulled on her thong underwear, the dragon's tail whipped like it was alive, its claws creeping under the thin waistband.

The woman caught Jenny staring and smiled at her, but Jenny, flustered, just pulled her towel tighter and stepped into a stall. She hadn't thought that a woman could be feminine, wear a thong, and work alongside men fighting fires. But why not? Although she never would have guessed such a tattoo existed under the hunter-green uniform pants.

She soaped up quickly, washed her hair, rinsed, and then got back into the safety of her towel as fast as she could. Jade was wrong: the disaster did not make Jenny feel any differently about showering in public.

When she walked back out to the lockers, the woman was loading her many pockets with radios and tightening her belt.

Jade cleared her throat.

'Do you know a firefighter named Nate?' she asked.

The woman tilted her head. 'Nate?' She had curly jet-black hair that glistened all around her face, which was tanned from working outside. 'There's about four hundred people working this blaze now, so I'm not sure. I might know him, but he's not in my crew.'

'Oh, of course. That makes sense,' said Jenny.

'A crush?'

'Oh God, no. He just found my cat, so I was hoping to thank him.'

Jenny was getting cold standing there in her towel and wished she hadn't said anything.

'I can call on my radio,' said the woman, holding it up.

'No, no, that's not necessary.'

'Okay, if you're sure?'

'Yes, definitely. So do you think we'll get to go back home soon?' She didn't want to leave the woman with the impression that she was looking for Nate like some kind of stalker.

'Depends on when we can get solid containment. You don't live in the Canyon, do you?'

'No, we're on the east side of town, actually.'

'Oh, you're lucky. We lost forty houses in the Canyon. There was just no way to stop it.'

'That's terrible,' said Jenny. She had heard they'd lost thirty. The number was going up.

'I know. I hate coming in here to shower and running into people from there. I feel so guilty. But luckily, no deaths.'

'Well, people don't blame you, do they?'

'I think people always want someone to blame in a tragedy. And that wacko with the illegal radio station really set us back.'

'Coyote Jones? He's not a wacko.'

It was just a gut reaction, but Jenny immediately sensed she'd hit a nerve defending him.

'Okay, well, I have to go do the briefing. Nice to meet you.'

'People really trust him,' Jenny said quickly. 'It's just, you know, he's local and everything. And his signal reaches into three states . . .'

Did the woman just raise an eyebrow?

'I mean, nobody knows him personally. But he's been our go-to guy for years for everything – storms, fires, weird weather fronts . . .'

Why was she trying so hard to make a point about Coyote Jones? She was acutely aware of being naked under her towel and her teeth were starting to chatter, but for some reason she kept talking.

'I mean, yeah, he's not FCC legal or anything, but you're all kind of on the same side. We're really appreciative, I promise.'

'We can't have conflicting information. If we say go and he says stay, somebody's going to get hurt.'

Jenny wished she'd kept quiet.

'You're freezing. If I meet Nate, I'll tell him you're looking for him.'

'Oh, please don't. I don't even know him.'

The woman cocked her head again, then shrugged and said, 'Well, I hope you get to go home soon. Sounds like your house will make it. Nice to meet one of the lucky ones.'

One of the lucky ones, Jenny thought as she dressed.

She felt like the woman was holding back, as if she'd wanted to enlighten Jenny about what was really going on.

She pictured how disappointed Jade and her friends would be when the person leading the briefing turned out to be a woman instead of the dishy guy they were hoping for. *A woman with a dragon on her ass who hates Coyote Jones*, Jenny thought, trying to make all those bits of information fit in her head.

She pushed the door open and ran smack into a firefighter coming out of the men's locker room with a towel over his head and scissors in his hand.

'Oops! Whoa, careful – I almost impaled you.'

'Oh, hey!'

'Wow, what are the odds of running into you, Miss Scarlett?'

'It's Jenny. And thank you for saving my cat.'

'Jenny, hi. I'm Nate.'

'What happened to your face?'

'It ran into the claws of a very scared cat.'

'Oh no, Colonel Mustard did that? I'm so sorry.'

'It's fine. I was dragging him out of what he thought was a safe place, so I don't blame him.'

'Was it safe?'

'Well, as long as the fire didn't reach your laundry basket.'

'I'm just heading over to see him.'

'I bet that will make him feel better.'

'I really am sorry.'

'Got a minute?' He held up the scissors. 'I need to go very, very short.'

When she'd met him, his hair had been hidden

under a hard hat. But now it hung down like thick vines around his face, which was no longer covered in soot. He wasn't much older than she was.

'I thought I could just tie it back all summer, but it's a pain in the ass. Also dangerous. Crew boss says to cut it.'

'I don't know anything about cutting hair.'

'But you know how to work a pair of scissors?'

'Yeah, if you don't care how it looks.'

'I was just going to do it myself, so the bar isn't very high. And besides, I wear a hard hat ninety percent of the time.'

'Okay, if you're sure.'

It was awkward as hell. Jenny knew that if Jade were following a firefighter outside to sit on a log and cut his beautiful hair, she would be flirting and carrying the conversation as if she'd known him forever. But Jenny was dying to get back to Colonel Mustard.

'You know, my sister would be much better at this.'

'Cutting hair?'

'Well, probably that too. No – talking, flirting, whatever this is …' *Way to go Jenny, batting a thousand here.*

'Um, not flirting, if that's what you think.'

'Yeah, no, I just meant … Oh God, I'm sorry. Whatever. I don't know what I'm saying.'

He laughed. 'Relax. I joined the Forest Service to forget a girl, not find one. You're perfectly safe.'

He had the towel across his shoulders and was sitting on the log with his back to her.

'Okay, just strike everything stupid I said from the record,' said Jenny.

'Already gone,' he said.

'Well, are you ready?' She made a couple of snipping sounds near his head.

'Please just don't chop off my ear.'

If she were Jade, she might mention Van Gogh and the idea of mailing a severed ear to one's love interest. But again: not Jade.

She picked up a thick chunk of hair.

'Still okay?'

'Yeah, but not if you keep asking.'

One snip and it hung limp in her hand. She waved it in front of his eyes, but he said nothing. She thought he might be holding his breath.

'So tell me about the girl you're trying to forget. I mean, if you want to.'

But he talked about firefighting instead. The long hours, the food, the adrenaline rush. She kept snipping away, trying to focus on his words rather than on the intimacy of his hair between her fingers, smelling like burnt toast.

'I was hoping to get on a crew as a smoke jumper in Alaska.'

'Alaska?'

'Well, it would have gotten me farther away from home. You know, from things I'm trying to forget.'

He changed the subject.

'I have a twin brother who's in Alaska at a summer camp.'

But Jenny was stuck on what he'd said before. 'Things I'm trying to forget.'

Jade's stupid umbrella.

If that umbrella didn't exist, Jenny wouldn't have been reminded of its significance. It was like a portal between what might have happened to Jade and how that event had shaped them, defined them.

Every time Jenny thought about that stranger saying 'Just come through these trees with me,' she felt sick. For years she'd thought Jade was lying. But what if Jade had actually followed him into those woods?

Jenny wanted to feel relieved that her sister hadn't been hurt or vanished, like that other little girl. Finding the umbrella had made it all feel real again.

If only Jade didn't suck all the air out of the room, maybe things would be different between them.

'Am I boring you?' asked Nate.

'Oh no, not at all.' What had she missed? 'So are you and your twin identical in every way?' she asked, hoping it wasn't too off topic.

'Just looks. We're actually pretty different.'

'Well, maybe you don't look identical anymore. I think I'm done.'

He faced her, running a hand over his head, making the little bit of hair he had left all spiky. His ears stuck out at odd angles, not at all symmetrical. Jenny tried to arrange her features into a neutral expression.

'Okay, well, no mirror, so by the look on your face, is it that bad?'

'No, just ... Wow. It's pretty short.'

Her haircut hadn't done him any favours.

'My sister and I have a complicated relationship too,' she said, surprising herself. 'I mean, we aren't twins or anything, but she has this way of attracting so much attention, I feel invisible most of the time.'

It was the first time Jenny had ever said that to anyone, and she was grateful that he just nodded as if she made perfect sense.

It was intoxicating, being honest for once, even with a stranger. Or maybe especially with a stranger.

When his face had been covered in soot, she'd only noticed the whites of his eyes, but now she could tell the irises were a forest green that changed shades in the light, like a mood ring. It surprised her, this tiny detail, or perhaps the fact that she'd noticed it at all. One of the scratches on his cheek stood out now too, a thin crevasse in his skin that had opened as he talked and was pulsing with little beads of bright red blood.

Without thinking, she ran a finger lightly down the length of his cut. 'I'm really sorry Colonel Mustard did that to you.'

'Wow, Jenny. Are you going to introduce us to your friend?'

Jade's voice hit her like an arrow in the back of the head.

And of course the giggling was coming from Shelby and Carly, because they were like Charlie's Angels, always together and sniffing out gossip.

Jenny turned stiffly toward them, but not before she saw the look on Nate's face: Confusion? Relief? Had she really just caressed his scratch?

Jade was staring at the wispy piles of hair scattered near their feet, as if a strawberry-blond sheep had just been sheared. Jenny waited for her sister to say something witty and Jade-like, but she seemed to be at a loss for words.

'Jade, this is Nate. He actually found Colonel Mustard for us. Nate, my sister, Jade.'

Whose timing couldn't be worse.

Nate stood up and reached out a hand to Jade, then nodded hello to Shelby and Carly, like a proper gentleman.

He pulled the towel off his shoulders and shook it out.

'So thanks for the haircut. I should get back to base camp.'

He seemed in a hurry to get away.

From me, thought Jenny. *Why did I touch his face like that?*

'Going to see Colonel Mustard,' Jenny said to Jade and her friends, turning quickly in the opposite direction, grateful when nobody followed her. She was almost at the animal shelter when she realised she was still carrying the scissors.

The makeshift shelter was a cacophony of barks and meows and high, piercing animal sounds that made it hard to think, which was fine with Jenny.

'Can I just take my cat's kennel with me? He seems really freaked out in here.'

She'd tapped someone on the shoulder. When the woman turned around, she was face to face with the dragon lady again.

'Oh, hi.'

'Hey. I don't actually have anything to do with the animals.'

'Right. Sorry.'

'But did you see the news?'

Jenny brightened. 'No … do we get to go back home?'

'Oh no, not that. It's something else.'

She handed Jenny a clipping from the *Rocky Mountain News*.

'Everyone's talking about it,' she said. 'I've got to

run now.' Her radio was making a staticky noise. 'And I guess I should say sorry. I know you all trusted him.'

But her finger was in one ear and her radio was in the other, and she was gone so fast, Jenny got the impression that she didn't want to stay and watch her read the article. At the same time, Jenny had the distinct feeling that this was why the dragon lady had given her such a strange look in the locker room. She'd already known.

BODY SUSPECTED TO BE THAT OF GIRL MISSING FOR TWO YEARS
Suspect in Custody

Local celebrity and longtime weatherman Earl Jackson, known to radio listeners as Coyote Jones, has been charged with the abduction and murder of a six-year-old girl who went missing in the forest near her home two years ago. To protect the family's privacy, the girl's name is not being released at this time. The investigation is ongoing, and more charges are pending.

Jenny didn't ask anyone if she could take Colonel Mustard and his kennel with her; she just did it. She wanted to get away from all the noise and bury her face in her cat's fur. It was the only thing that made sense.

This was going to be too much for her mother, who

had believed in Coyote Jones, just like everybody else. Small-town trust is the backbone of small-town living. But it was unravelling.

Before this latest article, people in the shelter had been grappling with news that the fire had actually been started by a priest way over in Granville. Her mother's eye twitch had gotten worse when they heard this. She had been raised Catholic and said that was reason enough for her girls not to be.

'What those men get away with . . .' she said to Jenny and Jade mysteriously. 'One day the whole church is going to implode, and I, for one, am not going to be one bit surprised.'

As their mother watched them take Father Lazaria away in the big black car on the news, her eye twitch had been working overtime. He was being sent to a retirement home, where he would no longer be a danger to himself or society.

'Oh, that's how they deal with it,' her mother had said. 'I don't care what they tell you on the news, I'll bet my good eye setting a fire in a dumpster isn't the worst thing he's ever done.'

This coming from a woman who had almost lost her house.

Now Jenny wondered: Was Coyote Jones the same man who had given Jade the five-dollar bill?

'Jenny, there you are.' *Oh, speak of the devil.*

'Did you hear?' Jenny asked Jade, holding up the article. She didn't want to talk about it, but she also didn't want to talk about Nate and the hair cutting.

'I did.'

'Did you see his picture?'

'Yeah. I honestly can't remember if he's the same one I saw.'

'You're not going to just make something up, though, say it was him anyway?'

'Why would I do that?'

'Sorry, I didn't mean it.'

Jenny was so flustered by all this new information, she wasn't choosing her words very well.

'You don't believe me, do you?'

'No, Jade, that's not what I meant.'

But Jade was now staring at Jenny, as if they'd just met for the first time and she wasn't sure what to believe.

'I was six,' Jade said. 'And I did like the attention. But I never lied, Jenny.'

'I'm sorry, Jade. I didn't mean it.'

'I think you did.'

'Okay, I did. I just . . . God, that was so mean of me. And now that little girl has just been found and I'm sort of freaking out and I'm so sorry. I can be so awful. I'm really glad that didn't happen to you, I swear.'

'It was a long time ago. You have no idea how sick I

am of the whole thing. We should just get over it. Can we do that?'

'Definitely. Done,' said Jenny.

Jade looked at Colonel Mustard in the kennel. She reached in to stroke his nose with the tip of her finger.

'That girl's family is going to have to deal with this all over again,' said Jenny quietly.

Jade nodded. Mostly she just looked sad. 'That guy you were with, he came by looking for you.'

'Nate?'

'Yeah, he said he had to leave and asked me to give you this note. He seems nice.'

'He is nice.'

Jade gave her a sideways glance.

'I'll take Colonel Mustard back to our cots if you want,' she said, to change the subject. 'He looks really traumatised.'

'Like all of us,' said Jenny.

'Yeah, like all of us,' Jade agreed.

She waited until Jade was out of sight before opening Nate's note.

Hey Jenny,

Thanks for the haircut. Sorry I was a bit nervous about the scissors. Just wanted to say goodbye, we're moving west with the fire. You guys can go back home soon.

It's none of my business, so take this with a grain of salt, but I don't think your sister upstages you at all. I noticed you and I haven't noticed anyone new in four years.

Give my regards to Colonel Mustard. Look me up if you ever find yourself in Pigeon Creek. Just leave a note on the bulletin board at the Duck-In and I'll get it. It's a small town.

All the best,

Nate

There's Gas in the Tank, Louise!

'Do you think it was because of her boots?'

Addie is lying on Louise's bed, walking her dirty feet up the wall.

'Who?' asks Louise, even though she knows perfectly well who.

'Mom,' says Addie. 'And Dad. The yellow boots.'

'Don't be ridiculous,' says Louise.

'They went on a second honeymoon – gross, by the way – and then they get home and can barely talk to each other,' says Addie. 'Was it because of the ugly boots, and are they going to split up?'

'People don't split up over boots,' says Louise.

'Why not?'

'They just don't.'

'They could.'

'No, they could not.'

'Remember when you said people's backs don't go out because they bend over to pick up the shampoo? And then wham-o! Out went Dad's back in the shower.'

'It's called the last straw.'

'No, it was shampoo. Head and Shoulders,' says Addie.

'The shampoo was the last straw,' says Louise, trying to concentrate on putting on her mascara.

'So the ugly boots could have been the last straw?' asks Addie.

'I don't know. Will you please get a washrag and wipe your dirty footprints off my wall?'

'If I don't, will it be the last straw?'

Louise considers this, holding her eye open with her left hand, trying not to impale herself with the mascara brush in her right.

She has a long fuse for Addie, all things considered.

'Maybe,' she says.

Addie snorts disbelievingly.

'You're funny, Louise.'

'Please just clean up the wall, in case Mom comes in here.'

That does it. Addie jumps up and goes into the jack-and-jill bathroom that separates their rooms. Their sisters, Gladys and Isabelle, have another jack-and-jill bathroom that separates theirs, but they've both gone off to college and don't come home very often. Louise told Addie she should use the other bathroom – they could each have their own – but Addie says she likes sharing with Louise.

Four girls and twenty years of marriage.

Louise doesn't even want to think about her parents and which straw might have been the last one.

She understands complexity and how to ignore things in a way that Addie does not. Her parents didn't go on a second honeymoon. It was a Hail Mary trip, intended to save their crumbling marriage. Louise knows Addie has realised she was the surprise baby that came along eight years after her parents were supposedly done having children.

She tends to be overly sensitive about that at times.

'Mom threw them in the back of the closet and swore at them,' Addie says, dripping a sopping-wet washcloth all the way across Louise's room.

'So what, maybe they gave her blisters.'

'She said the whole trip was ruined because of them.'

'Because of blisters?'

'No, because of the boots, Louise.'

Addie snaps her fingers twice near Louise's head, a gesture her father often uses when he's trying to get his daughters to 'wake up and listen'.

'I heard her slamming drawers and throwing things into the closet, saying she didn't care anymore, the boots had ruined her bleepity-bleepity-bleepity-bleeping trip.'

'Whoa.'

'Right?' Addie is pleased that news of her mother

swearing has made Louise stop fussing with her eyelashes for half a second.

'What did she say after that?'

'She said something about how she hated Seattle, the people, the rain, all of it.'

Louise goes back to her mascara. She hadn't understood why they'd chosen Seattle for a second honeymoon. But she could care less what her parents did anyway.

'Speaking of straws, I heard we shouldn't use them anymore. One day they're going to find one in the nose of a turtle. Plastic will destroy the world.'

Where does she come up with this stuff? Just keep talking, Addie. I am so out of here.

'Are you going over to Finn Carson's?' Addie asks, smearing muddy water all over Louise's wall.

'None of your beeswax,' says Louise, wondering if Addie is telepathic.

Yes, I am going over to Finn Carson's and I'm going to lose the rest of my virginity, not that you need to know that.

'I heard that earwax can actually make you go deaf if you let it build up.'

Good. Not telepathic.

Louise should have known that her putting mascara on right before bed would not go unnoticed by her attentive little sister. But in spite of Addie's tornado personality, Louise knows she would never tell.

The real challenge is not being noticed on the other end, at Finn's house. He has six brothers, and one of them is a real pain in Louise's ass. Finn's twin, Nate. Of course the boy she likes would have a twin. Her elder sisters hadn't had to deal with that when they each fell for one of the Carson boys, the twinless ones.

With seven boys in the Carson house and four girls in hers, Louise is aware that sneaking over to the Carsons' has become a bit of a cliché. She'd like to do something that isn't seen as following in her sisters' footsteps, but what choice does she have when the only path to anything exciting is the one they've created?

The next most exciting thing Louise and her sisters ever did was get really, really good at tp-ing houses. They called it Charmin bombing. They did it *a lot*. Louise could encircle entire carports without breaking the roll. Gladys could do a fifty-foot tree without a ladder or a boost. Izzy somehow did the insides of houses while people slept, and they would not wake up. She left her initials on their cheeks and drew moustaches on them with red lipstick and still never once got caught.

Addie hasn't figured out what she might be good at yet.

The McQuillen sisters are proof that in a small town, teenagers are *always* and *never* bored.

Mr Carson loved that he never had to buy toilet

paper – thanks to Louise and her sisters he'd acquired hundreds of rolls, probably, over the years. He put it in his bathroom, wrapping it into fat loops that looked like giant fluffy rolls of cotton candy next to the toilet.

'Give me back my goddamn toilet paper,' Louise's father would demand, standing in the church parking lot, lowering his voice because the statue of Mary was nearby, eyeing him askance from under her blue veil.

'I believe it's on my property, and you have a bigger problem than toilet paper if you can't keep your daughters in line,' Mr Carson would bark back at him, also glancing at Mary.

It was all part of their routine, their shtick while smoking cigarettes after Mass. Louise's father complaining that with four girls he went through a hell of a lot of toilet paper, even when he wasn't chasing it around the neighbourhood; Mr Carson saying he couldn't help it if Mr McQuillen's daughters and toilet paper always ended up at his house.

It was a crumbling town, held loosely together by these routines and miles and miles of toilet paper hung in the trees like prayer flags. Catholics aren't normally ones to summon God with prayer flags, but Louise figured they needed whatever help they could get.

'Louise?'

Addie's fingers are shaking her gently by the shoulder.

'What time is it? Oh, no, no, no, no.'

'Coyote Jones says there's a wildfire over near Beaver Junction.'

Louise rolls over to find Addie's face so close she can smell her bubble-gum-flavoured toothpaste.

'That's not very close,' she says. 'Your face, however, that's close. You are a fire in my face.'

'I can smell smoke.'

'I just smell toothpaste.'

'I think you should stay home.'

'I am home. I was asleep.'

Dammit, how could she have fallen asleep?

'But you were planning to leave.'

Addie knowingly plucks the collar of Louise's corduroy jacket. Her sneaking-out jacket.

Louise wishes she had more secrets. Better secrets. Any secrets.

'I was cold.'

'You won't be when the fire gets here.'

'It's not going to get here.'

'Should we fill up the gas tank?'

'What? Why?'

'In case we have to evacuate quickly.'

'It's winter, Addie. There is no fire.'

'A fire can burn uphill at forty miles per hour.'

'Stop listening to Coyote Jones. He's bad for your mental health. Now go back to bed.'

'He knows things,' Addie whispers icily in Louise's ear, making her shiver.

When she opens her eyes, Addie is gone.

On her way out, carrying her boots and sliding along quietly in her socks, Louise pauses by Addie's door, leaning her ear against it. She should peek in and make sure Addie isn't mad or worried, but she's already so late. Finn must think she's blown him off. Addie's probably asleep, anyway; it's deathly quiet on the other side of the door. Either that or she's still tuned in to Coyote Jones's radio channel in her big fat headphones. Louise has always thought the self-proclaimed weather guy was a quack. She moves guiltily past.

She shuffles even more quietly past the closed door to Gladys's room, because that's where her father sleeps now, ever since the 'second honeymoon'. Louise misses her sisters more than she misses her parents getting along, which she honestly can't remember.

Sisters shouldn't leave their sisters. It sounds like a bumper sticker, but it feels like a bee sting to the brain. Louise has already decided not to move away when she graduates, because she wouldn't do that to Addie.

She figures she can get a job waitressing at the Duck-In – she could work nights – and maybe Finn will stay too and work for his father's plumbing business. In her mind, it looks like a diorama, the kind Addie makes out of shoe boxes with little figurines glued down, all spit-spot. Very neat. As if living in miniature is less messy than life-sized. Even the tiny plastic toilets she puts in the bathrooms never have to be cleaned. That's a life Louise can see herself living.

'Why so many dioramas?' she'd asked, looking at the twenty different-sized shoe boxes all over Addie's room. The box the yellow boots had come in was the biggest, and Addie was making a tiny replica of their town out of it. Louise recognised their house and the Carsons', and the path that led between them. Beyond it were all the right angles that connected the streets of Pigeon Creek. The school, the sledding hill, their church, and the Duck-In, decorated with Christmas lights and a sign that said open 24 hours, just like in real life.

'I like to recycle,' said Addie. 'Someday people will realise it's important.'

'Yeah, but it's so ... extensive. And detailed.'

'I notice things.'

'Really?'

'No, Louise, I'm actually a human drone, and this is what you all look like from my perspective.'

'Just asking. Don't get all panty bunched about it.'

When Louise peered closer she saw that the Nike box that was their house had five little plastic people – two parents, three kids – inside. Her dad had stopped running at least ten years ago, so the box was flimsy

227

and old. The people were all seated around a kitchen table with what looked like roast chicken made of foil smack-dab in the middle of it. She couldn't remember the last time her family had sat down together for dinner.

On the tablecloth there were dishes drawn with markers and little Tater Tots made of broken bits of wine corks rolling around inside them. A ketchup bottle the size of Louise's thumbnail was standing nearby. In the bedrooms, every bed had a comforter made of a Bounce dryer sheet cut in half and then decorated with flowers drawn with brightly coloured markers, made to look like the ones they all slept under every night. It was astounding how lifelike everything was.

'So these aren't, like, voodoo dolls of us, are they?'

'You're ridiculous.'

'There's only five people.'

Addie was focused on making a tiny vase, and she was uncharacteristically quiet.

Louise double-checked the bathrooms on the second floor in case a tiny plastic figurine was in there, constipated or something (that would so be Addie's speed). She slid open the cardboard pocket door to an exact replica of the bathroom she and Addie shared. But it was empty. She admired the intricately designed sink and shower and tiny rolls of toilet paper – Certs candies – stacked neatly on the back of the toilet.

'Is one of us over in the Carsons' house? That's very clever, Addie.'

She looked at the huge yellow rain-boot box that was their town, but it didn't show the insides of any of the houses, just long strands of real toilet paper connecting all the buildings.

'Someone's missing, Addie.'

'Stop it, Louise. You overthink everything.'

Addie put her hand on her hip and stuck out her elbow like a handle before Louise could say anything else.

'Nice to meet you, Pot. I'm Kettle.'

Then she bowed deeply at the waist.

Louise groaned.

'Are you ever going to grow up?' she asked.

'Doesn't seem likely,' said Addie.

Louise's feet feel heavier than usual as she makes her way to Finn's, glancing over her shoulder in case Addie has decided to follow. But she wouldn't. She never does.

Her sneaking-out jacket isn't really warm enough now that it's snowing. The conversation about a wildfire smoulders in the back of her mind, the way a real fire would smoulder this time of year. It felt more like an excuse for Addie to keep Louise home.

Gladys and Izzy had a rule about the car that the

girls all shared: Don't fill it up more than halfway, so that way if you crash and total it you won't have wasted money on unused gas. But never leave less than half a tank in it for the next person either.

They would pass each other on the stairs and whisper ominously, 'The tank is half full,' winking as if they shared a deep, dark secret.

Now that Gladys and Izzy are gone, Louise often leaves it with a quarter tank or less, since she's the only driver. It's an old Toyota hatchback with almost three hundred thousand miles on it that needs a Phillips screwdriver rather than a key to start. Her feet are more reliable. And she rarely needs to go anywhere that she can't walk, anyway.

Louise misses her sisters more than she allows herself to acknowledge, but walking over to Finn's, shivering in her thin jacket, she feels too exposed to fight it and lets herself wallow for a few minutes in the loneliness of being left behind. In her pocket is a condom Izzy 'bequeathed' her when she left.

'Those Carson boys are never prepared,' she'd said to Louise knowingly. 'And while they are a fun distraction, you do not want to hitch your wagon to them forever. Trust me.'

Izzy had been hopelessly in love with the eldest Carson, Jeremiah, and Louise wondered two things about her sister's sage advice: Had Izzy really not wanted to be hitched to his wagon forever? And did he pass on some intimate knowledge of 'those McQuillen girls' to his brothers, the way her sisters had done for her?

Gladys had said, 'The McQuillen–Carson pipeline. Don't even bother signing up. All roads lead to the same place.' Still, she tossed one of those black-and-white photo strips of herself and Markus, the third eldest, into her suitcase when she left. Louise noticed that Gladys hadn't packed any pictures of her and Addie, so she'd slipped one into the side pocket of her sister's bag when she wasn't looking. Addie was about six and had ice cream all over her face. Louise was fourteen and too old to be wearing a holster and riding a stick horse that was way too small for her. It always made Addie laugh when Louise wore her dress-up clothes, so she did it a lot. It's also what Louise likes most about the picture – Addie laughing.

The photo booth sits in the back corner of the Duck-In like a time machine, documenting the late-night mischief of a small town's teenagers through the years. Louise even had the same requisite Carson–McQuillen black-and-white photo strip – of herself and Finn – which made her feel boring and predictable. (Except that Nate had stuck his hand through the curtain and given them bunny ears, because he was also boring and predictable.)

Nate was not just her boyfriend's twin brother; he was a constant shadow, a monkey on Louise's back. He taunted her with his presence, his simmering jealousy about her and Finn. She wondered who he thought would be better for his brother, if not her? Cindy Trout, the one they called 'the fish'? Or triangle-shaped Claudia Klein, with her big swimming shoulders? Or that new girl, Martha Hollister? She seemed to be on a mission to date every boy in Pigeon Creek before the year ended. Why didn't Nate just date one of them himself? Louise didn't know, because she rarely spoke to him, and yet she knew his moods like she knew Addie's.

She knew his twisted downward grimace or the hundred-mile stare with the same hazel-green eyes that Finn had, except Nate's were moodier. Louise would beg Finn to do something that was just the two of them, without Nate, but the only time that ever happened was if they were making out in the closet in the room the two boys shared. It was uncomfortable and sweaty – she had been jabbed more than once by a stray hanger – not at all romantic, the way Izzy and Gladys had described their jaunts at this particular rodeo.

But Finn had promised her that tonight it would just be the two of them. *And I fell asleep on this night of all nights*, she thinks, dribbling dog treats along the fence next door to the Carsons' for the Dobermann that lives there. (*Thank you, Gladys, for the heads-up.*)

It's as dark as the inside of a freezer. And almost as cold. She thinks about Addie warning her about wildfire. It's funny, but also not funny. Everything is a little off. Her lateness, Addie's plea for her not to go, no Dobermann coming out to get her dog treats.

And then something grabs her and she screams.

A hand covers her mouth and she's pulled off the trail into the woods.

'Shhhhh. You'll wake the whole world.'

Goddammit, Nate.

'I'm trying to help you. Stop it, Louise.'

But she twists madly, trying to get out of his grasp. He's twice her size, in height and weight. She bites the hand that's covering her mouth.

'Shit, Louise! What the fuck?'

Her mouth is free now, but he's still holding her in a tight bear hug.

'I'll scream again if you don't let me go.'

'If you do, that's it, goddammit. I'm done with you.'

'Well, that's an incentive.'

But what does being 'done with her' mean? And it's very odd that he was waiting in the woods.

'What the hell is going on?' she asks.

'Let's go to the Duck-In and I'll tell you everything.'

'Finn is waiting for me.'

'I promise you, Finn is not waiting. He sent me here to meet you.'

'You've really gone too far this time, Nate. I'm going inside.'

'He's got another girl in there, Louise. And if you go inside, you're going to humiliate yourself.'

She stares at him. It's so dark, he could easily just be one of the black spruce trees leaning up against her, his long arms branches clutching her shoulders through her thin jacket. She looks up at the fingernail moon smirking at her in the black sky ... She was meeting Finn for something else; he'd agreed to meet her ... What was it? Addie, telling her there was a fire – had she known something too? But how?

'So did Finn give you something for me?'

'Come on, let's go to the Duck-In.'

Louise doesn't remember moving her feet, but somehow she is sitting across from Nate at the Duck-In. As she starts to thaw out, everything hurts, but especially her pride. Not that anyone else is in the cafe to notice. It's so bright inside she feels exposed all the way down to her core, like the empty skeleton hanging in her biology class – a bony cage with nothing inside except her heart. It must be visible, trying to pump blood to the rest of her body, as if the ventricles were a sponge being wrung out. Maybe it won't spring back into shape, the way it's supposed to, and she will die across from Nate Carson, in a crappy diner booth with syrup sticking to her ass.

Nate orders two coffees with cream, and extra sugar for Louise, as if they do this all the time.

If he's gloating that Finn had someone else in his room, she doesn't get why he brought her here to do it. His long legs bump the table as he shifts around in the booth, jostling their coffees, spilling cream everywhere.

'I can't do it anymore,' he says.

'Okayyyy . . .'

She thaws her fingers over the steam rolling off her coffee cup.

'Don't you want to know what "it" is?'

Not really, she thinks. 'He invited me over tonight. Why would he do that if someone else was going to be there?'

'He didn't actually invite you over, Louise.'

She looks up into his face, surprised to see that it doesn't hold one ounce of smugness. He pulls off his red knitted cap, running long, slender fingers through short hair.

It's a drastic change from the Grizzly Adams look he's always had. When was the last time Louise even looked at Nate? How long has his hair been short?

'Louise, you have to stop this.'

'What?'

'You guys broke up almost two years ago.'

235

'That's ridiculous.'

'I think you need to talk to someone.'

'I talk to Addie all the time.'

The look on his face is so full of love and concern, she thinks she might cry. God damn him, making her talk. Making her say Addie's name out loud.

She's suddenly so exhausted she can't hold her head up. She doesn't even care that her cheek is pressing against dirty Formica that smells like old soup; she just wants to melt into the table and let the Jackson Five sing her to sleep with their lousy rendition of 'I Saw Mommy Kissing Santa Claus' bleating out of the old jukebox.

'I called your sisters a few days ago,' he says.

Or she thinks he says it, but she is half dreaming now.

She and Addie are playing follow-the-leader in the woods. 'Be as quiet as you can,' she tells Addie. 'If I hear you at all, then you lose and we switch places, until one of us is queen.'

Addie is so good at this game. Louise leads them through the dry sagebrush and doesn't even hear Addie's sneakers on the path behind her. She keeps going, sure Addie will give herself away, but minutes go by and there's not even a giggle. She keeps going, into the dense alders, and still Addie is quiet, determined to win. Louise knows she will have to give in and declare

Addie queen for the day, but she decides to walk just a bit farther, to the money bear, the stump that looks like a baby bear, where people leave coins if they have them. There's always a dime or a nickel stashed in the wooden grooves when the girls get there.

'You win!' Louise shouts, pulling a quarter – big-money day! – from the money bear's gnarled paw and turning to hand it to her sister. No Addie.

For the hundredth time tonight, someone is shaking her shoulders. Her face feels glued to the table, and it takes all her strength to lift her head. She can smell fresh coffee, sees two more cups being set down by Maeve, the waitress who has known them all since forever. Tonight she has a red streak in her hair and a look of concern as she softly runs a hand over Louise's head, then turns back to the kitchen.

Louise tries to focus.

'Gladys? What are you doing here?'

'I'm here too, bug,' says Izzy. Her sisters look huge, standing next to the table.

'She's been – I don't know – imagining things, or talking about things that aren't real,' Nate is saying. 'She thinks Addie's home, telling her not to go out. She doesn't seem to remember that she and Finn aren't together anymore.'

'Shouldn't you two be in school?' says Louise.

Gladys and Izzy slide into the booth and Louise

feels an arm around her shoulders, smells oranges, because Izzy always smells like oranges.

'I'm fine,' she mumbles. 'What is this, some kind of intervention?'

'You don't look fine,' says Gladys.

'Yeah, I'm a drug addict,' says Louise. It's a joke. Nobody laughs.

'We know,' says Izzy. 'We found your stash.'

'A few pills. God, Izzy, "stash"? Seriously.'

'Not that you were trying to hide it or anything. All those shoe boxes full of pill bottles, stuffed into your old doll houses?'

'Those are dioramas,' says Louise, putting her head back on the table. *And they're not mine, they're Addie's.*

'Is she going to be okay?' Nate asks.

'She needs help,' Izzy says. 'We're getting her treatment. God, Nate, thank you so much for calling us.'

Nate has been spying on me?

'I have to go home. Addie's waiting . . .' She didn't mean to say it out loud.

'Shhh, honey, Addie isn't at home. You know this. She was missing for two years, Louise. They just found her body in August.'

Gladys is crying. Izzy is crying. Louise is beginning to hear what they're saying, which means she needs another pill, just to take the edge off. She does not want to live in the real world, where her little sister was about to be queen for a day and then disappeared forever. All because of Louise.

Her parents are splitting up because they can't handle it anymore, and maybe Finn doesn't want to be her boyfriend either, because who would? Has it really been two years since they split up? He must have told Nate all her secrets.

'I was sick of watching him let you numb yourself to death,' says Nate. 'I don't care if you hate me, Louise, this is killing me. The way everyone pretends nothing is happening and the world just falls apart around you. I'm sorry. I had to do something.'

He is incredibly serious as he unwraps Louise's fingers from the coffee mug and then rewraps both his hands over hers. She stares at the familiar curve of his thumb, the bitten-down nails, the brown semicircle birthmark on his left knuckle, exactly like the one Finn has on his right. Two halves of a full moon.

Tom Petty is blaring through the speakers because Maeve, in her Maeve way, has surreptitiously turned up the music.

You belong among the wildflowers.

'Were you in Alaska or something?' she asks, pulling a vague memory from somewhere.

'No, not Alaska. You're thinking of Finn again. But thanks for noticing I was gone.'

He's actually laughing, but there's also a real tear streaming down his cheek, or is that a scar that she's never seen before?

'Don't be mad at Finn,' Louise says.

'I told him if he gives you any more pills I will kick his ass to the moon,' says Nate.

Gladys laughs, and the tension pops like a balloon.

'You win, Nate. You are the best Carson,' she says.

'And we are qualified to judge,' says Izzy.

Louise puts her head on the table again. She was grateful when Finn started giving her the pills, right after they found Addie's body. Everyone else had moved on to grieving, but Louise did not want to move on. She hears Addie telling her not to leave the house tonight. She knows she will never see Addie again, and her heart breaks for the millionth time since she lost her in the woods. Everyone, in their own way, has been left to make sense of something that can never be made sense of.

'You must blame me,' Louise whispers.

'Oh, bug.' Izzy is crying so hard she can barely speak. 'Nobody blames you. How could we? We all loved that game, especially Addie.'

Everyone is crying now, even Nate.

Sitting between her sisters makes Louise realise how much she has missed them. Not just for their advice about the Carson boys, or passing them on the stairs and hearing whispered assurances that the tank is half full. She has missed them because sisters should never leave their sisters.

'I didn't fill the tank,' says Louise. 'I didn't think you were coming back.'

Izzy lays her head on Louise's shoulder.

'We'll take my car,' says Gladys. 'And you'll never have to worry about being stranded all alone again, Louise. Ever.'

Acknowledgements

Hands down, my favourite character in this book is Elizabeth the invisible mermaid. Thanks to Rosie Fuller for introducing us; I tried hard to keep her alive. Rosie's mom, Maeve Conran, listened to me read way too many versions of these stories aloud, and I am so appreciative. Also, Sinead Fuller, thanks for naming Ruby, here and in real life.

Over the past few years, people gave me houses to work in, they lent me cars, took in my dog, brought me heating oil and wine and medical care (once). They taught me about marmots and bras that cause cancer, homemade toothpaste and what amnesic shellfish poisoning is. They took me on hikes and taught me about the flora and fauna of Colorado. And they read so many versions of bad stories, I'm sure they wondered if I'd ever write anything good. These people include, but are not limited to: Stacie and Chuck Power, Debbie Jo Rock, Colleen Hitchcock, Lori and Mike Cady, Loren Waxman, Susanne Larsen, Sam Rabung, Kendall Rock, Kathleen Glasgow, Ann Keala Kelly, Ann Dixon, Elizabeth Schoenfeld, Rebecca Grabill, Jessie Carlson, Bonnie Disalvo, Vicki Stegall, Garima Fairfax, Ken Aikin, Cheryl Van Der Horn, Bonnie Sullivan, Meg Johnson (Gramzy), and Chris Todd, who does so much more than bring me coffee, but he does that too. Arianna Sullivan, thanks for helping me try to find a Brecht scholar.

Suellen Nelles, Alison Jennings, Bonnie Powell, and all the counsellors from Camp Kushtaka 1989, thanks for the memories and the great material!

Thanks to the German band Parking Lot Flowers, who lent me their name and whose music I love.

William DeArmond read many of these stories before he passed away in 2017. An original member of The Squeaky Elbows and a true friend. I miss him dearly.

Thanks to the Alaska Fire Service and the Bureau of Land Management fire management teams that saved our place from the Shovel Creek Fire in the summer of 2019, inspiring more than a few details in 'The Stranger in the Woods'.

As always my agent, Molly Ker Hawn, is a godsend. The only reason this book exists is because she had faith in my desire to write a collection of short stories. Faith is a beautiful thing. Thank you, Molly.

Alice Swan, at Faber and Faber, whose keen eye never misses a chance to make me a better writer. Her work on this book was monumental, as if she knows when my brain is holding back and she just needs to stab it with a red-hot poker. I'm also very grateful to everyone at Faber who continues to support my books.

And a million thanks to my editor, Wendy Lamb. This is one of the last books she worked on before stepping down from her amazing imprint. I will savour every word, every edit, every hilarious email from her. I look forward to her freelance editorial life, and hope to be a part of it.

Many thanks as well to the whole Penguin Random House crew: Dana Carey, associate editor extraordinaire of Wendy Lamb Books; Adrienne Waintraub; Kristin Schulz in school and library marketing, Colleen Fellingham in copyediting, Tamar Schwartz in managing editorial, and the rest of the RHCB crew.

Special thanks to Dylan Hitchcock-Lopez, who always knows what I'm trying to say and can bluntly tell me when I haven't achieved it, even when he is short on time.

Thanks also to Sylvia Hitchcock-Jones, who gives

just the right amount of feedback, no extraneous fluff. I'd be so lost without these two.

Finally, 'Basketball Town' was inspired solely by my dad, who was a great coach and referee but an even better father. I miss him every day.

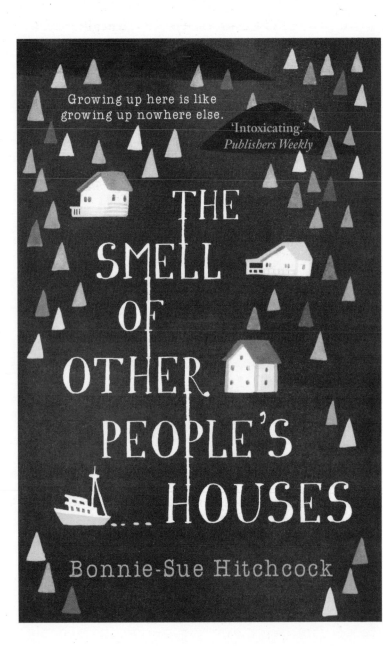

Growing up here is like
growing up nowhere else.

'Intoxicating.'
Publishers Weekly

THE
SMELL
OF
OTHER
PEOPLE'S
HOUSES

Bonnie-Sue Hitchcock